A ROGUE FOR CHRISTMAS

CHRISTMAS SCANDALS
BOOK THREE

SUZANNA MEDEIROS

A ROGUE FOR CHRISTMAS

If he was a better man, he'd stay far away from Iris Rowland. But no one had ever accused the Earl of Wentworth of being a good man.

After saving Iris from certain ruin, the unthinkable happens. He becomes obsessed with the memory of the young woman he rescued at the end of the season.

There is only one thing to do. Secure an invitation to the Christmas house party she'll be attending. But instead of putting his curiosity about Iris to rest, he is shocked to discover that his inconvenient attraction might be something more.

❄

To learn about Suzanna Medeiros's future books, you can sign up for her newsletter at suzannamedeiros.com/newsletter.

A Rogue for Christmas
First Digital Edition: November 2023
First Print Edition: November 2023
Cover design © Kim Killion
Edited by Victory Editing
ebook ISBN: 978-1-988223-52-0
Paperback ISBN: 978-1-988223-51-3

CHAPTER 1

December 1818

If he were a better man, he'd stay far away from Miss Iris Rowland. But no one had ever accused the Earl of Wentworth of being a good man. Which was why he'd gone out of his way to secure an invitation to Viscount Thornton's annual Christmas house party.

It was a calculated risk since he couldn't be certain Iris would be in attendance. But his discreet inquiries had shown this was his best course of action. His only path forward, really, if he didn't want to wait until the next season began before he could see her again.

It had been years since Wentworth had

ventured into the country for Christmas. Normally he spent the day in London, where he wouldn't have to listen to his mother's constant lectures about his unbecoming conduct. Staying in town also made it easier to conduct his affairs.

Not that he'd engaged in any liaisons of late, which was precisely the reason he was in Surrey. Iris Rowland was constantly in his thoughts—he'd even dreamed about her. Drastic action was needed to exorcise whatever spell she'd cast over him.

He'd only spoken to her once, and their encounter had been brief, but every second of their meeting out in the gardens during the last ball of the season was etched in his memory.

He'd grown bored early in the evening and made arrangements to meet an overeager new widow for a bit of fun. He'd been finding it increasingly difficult to enjoy his customary amusements of late and feared he was growing jaded. Hoping it was only a phase, he slipped out into the dimly lit gardens.

The moon wasn't positioned correctly to supply enough light that evening, and the large shrubs and flowering bushes cast dark shadows along the path. But light wasn't a requirement for what would happen tonight. One body was very much like another in the dark.

He blamed the shadows for his error in mistaking the woman standing in the garden for the buxom widow.

She was already waiting for him, facing away. He let out a sigh as he moved into place behind her. She was too old to make the mistake of turning her back on the path, where anyone could come across her.

He placed his arms on her hips and dragged her back into him. His mouth was already dropping to the exposed expanse of skin at the base of her neck when the unexpected happened. She raised her arm, but instead of reaching back to bury her fingers in his hair, she brought her elbow back sharply against his midsection.

It wasn't enough to hurt him, of course, but he released her at once. He enjoyed his dalliances, but he would never force a woman. Seduce her, yes, but he'd never use force. He was also annoyed that she was playing games with him. If this woman thought that he was going to chase her to get what he wanted, she would be sorely disappointed.

He was preparing to tell her just that as she

spun around to face him, but the admonition died on his lips.

Dammit, this wasn't the eager widow from the ballroom. No, the indignant young woman was the last person he'd expected to find here.

Iris Rowland. Sister-in-law to the Earl of Seaford and, from all indications, an innocent.

He watched the play of emotions cross her lovely face. Indignation, then shock. Her blue eyes widened, and her hands flew to her lips. Her cheeks were red, but he watched the color fade within moments.

"Oh! You're not—"

She seemed to think better of revealing who she'd planned to meet and snapped her lips closed.

"I take it you were expecting someone else?"

He thought she'd shake her head in denial. Perhaps babble some excuse and then flee. Instead, she folded her arms at her waist and frowned at him. The position framed her bodice, and he was powerless to stop his gaze from lowering to her breasts. Her bounty was more modest than the widow, but he found himself wondering how it would feel to drag this woman into his arms and make love to her.

"Are you quite done?"

He laughed. "You can cease playing the scandalized maiden, Miss Rowland. We both know why you are out here in the gardens late at night."

Her mouth dropped open, and then she glared at him. Actually glared. It was an amusing change of pace. Normally, women went out of their way to make themselves attractive—and available—to him. And young women newly out in society, well, they avoided him altogether.

But it seemed that Miss Rowland was made of sterner stuff. To his absolute shock, he was intrigued.

"You might be out here for other… nefarious reasons. But I just wanted to enjoy the gardens."

He crossed his arms, mimicking her stance, and held her gaze for several seconds. She looked away first.

She'd been angry that he'd dragged her against him, so perhaps she was telling the truth and thought that a man would meet her here late at night, alone, and not want to touch her.

"Who did you think I was when you spun around?"

Her lips firmed into a tight line, and he wanted to shake her. Surely her family didn't know she was sneaking out into the gardens to take in the flowers with some bloke who would think nothing of ruining her.

“You need to stay away from the gardens at night. They’re frequented by rogues and ne’er-do-wells.”

She lifted her chin, which somehow, despite the fact that he was at least a foot taller than her, had the effect of making it appear as though she were looking down at him. “Perhaps that was what I was seeking? Someone who wasn’t tame.”

He was fairly certain her demeanor was a show of bravado. Clearly Miss Rowland needed someone to shake her out of her complacency. To show her that the world wasn’t a safe place for gently bred young women.

He moved closer, aware of the way she drew him to her like a magnet. Normally he’d be putting as much space as possible between himself and someone who was fresh on the marriage mart.

“Are you looking for danger, Miss Rowland?”

Her eyes widened in surprise. “You know who I am?”

He held her gaze. “I make it a point to learn the identities of beautiful young women.”

Her head tilted to one side as she examined him. “I can’t decide whether that’s a genuine compliment or just something you say to all women."

He shrugged. "There are enough beautiful women in London that I don't need to lie to the ones who aren't."

She winced. "It's lowering to know that I'm just one of many."

He needed to step away from her. Instead, he moved closer and cupped her chin loosely. A surprising zing of attraction zipped up his arm. He couldn't remember the last time he'd been this intrigued by a woman.

"There is nothing ordinary about you."

Heat flooded her cheeks again. "Thank you."

He dropped his hand, but he didn't step away. He couldn't. "Who were you expecting, Iris?"

"Perhaps I was hoping that the infamous Lord Wentworth would see me slip away and follow me out here?"

He laughed, charmed despite himself by her bravado. "You're playing a dangerous game. What if I told you that was exactly what had happened? That I'd followed you out here, and now I want nothing more than to kiss you senseless."

She shied away then and took a step back. "Mr. Tobias Miller has been courting me. He told me that he wanted us to spend a few minutes alone together. I thought that perhaps he wanted to take our courtship further."

A haze of unexpected anger settled over him. He knew exactly what Miller wanted from Iris, and it wasn't to propose marriage. He kept his gaze focused on her, knowing that his next words would reveal the real reason behind Iris's foray into these gardens.

"I was at White's this morning. Miller was bragging about how he'd just offered for Miss Bennington and that his suit had been accepted."

All color drained from Iris's face. "I didn't know." She looked away, no doubt coming to the realization that Miller's proposal had not been the innocent one she'd expected.

"Do you care for him?" He had the irrational urge to find Miller and punch him.

She sighed, and he felt his heart constrict. He ignored the feeling. He didn't have a heart.

"No, which was why I decided to meet him here. I was going to tell him that it was probably best if he ceased his courtship." Her lips twisted in a wry grimace. "I thought that I was allowing myself to be unreasonable in my expectations, but there was something about him that set my teeth on edge. He seemed a little *too* solicitous."

Her response shouldn't have brought about the surge of relief flowing through him. "He's a bounder of the worst sort. A young woman like yourself doesn't expect to be led astray and taken advantage of."

"I was foolish coming out here. You're correct. I should go."

She started to move past him, but he'd caught the way her body shrank with shame. Anger surged through him that anyone would try to make this woman feel worthless. "I can call him out."

She froze, shocked at his statement. His outburst had surprised him as well.

She turned to face him and shook her head, those careful blond curls dancing about her face. He wondered what her hair would look like when she took it down that night before sliding under her covers. Would she let the mass tumble across the bedsheets, or would she carefully plait the strands to avoid tangles?

After staring at him for several seconds, she shook her head. "I don't know you. What would people say when word got out? People always whisper. Our names would be linked, and everyone would wonder..." She took a deep breath, and he was impressed by the way she took control over her obvious panic. "Thank you for the offer, my lord, but I think it best if I just return to the ballroom now."

He inclined his head. "Perhaps that would be best."

She gave him a tremulous smile. "I am in your debt, my lord."

Why did he want to take this young woman into his arms and tell her that he would protect her? She had protectors already. She knew that Seaford would kill any man who tried to take advantage of his wife's sister. He'd issued the warning himself at White's at the beginning of the season. But apparently Miller had a death wish.

Pushing aside the uncomfortable urge to protect Iris, he inclined his head. "Any true gentleman would do the same."

She sighed. "And now I must face him. He's going to approach me at some point this evening and ask me why I changed my mind about meeting him here."

"If he comes anywhere near you, simply smile and offer him felicitations on his betrothal."

That elicited a ghost of a smile. "I like the

sound of that. And then I'll make sure to spread the word about his upcoming marriage so he can't lure some other simpleton out into the gardens."

She was beginning to turn away again, but he couldn't let her leave this way.

"Iris."

She halted and turned back to face him. "Miller is a fool. You are worth ten, nay hundreds, of the other young women here. She has a great fortune to her name but little else to recommend her. You are beautiful and strong. Don't forget that."

She gave him a soft smile. "Never worry about that. When I'm finished spreading the word about how I overheard him trying to lure an unsuspecting victim for his debauchery into the gardens after he'd already offered for another…" She lifted one shoulder. "You are correct of course. I'm not the one who should be ashamed. Thank you for pointing that out."

"I am very happy to be of service."

And he was. He watched her go—and just in time. The widow entered the garden bower then, mere seconds after Iris had left. He winced as he thought about how the two would have crossed paths.

She threw herself into his arms, but his

thoughts were too full of the young woman he'd just saved from ruin. His mood had soured. And if he was being honest with himself, he'd much rather speak to Iris Rowland than lift the skirts of this woman whose name he didn't even know.

He pushed her away. "I'm afraid something has come up. I'm only here to tell you that we can't slip away together."

She pouted at him. "I've already said my good-byes. If you need to leave, perhaps you can join me in my carriage."

He watched how she leaned forward a little, giving him a tantalizing view of her breasts that were threatening to spill over the top of her dress. But the sight did little to entice him.

He needed to speak to Miller. Warn him away from Iris… from debauching any maiden, really, with false promises of a future he would never give them. That was the only reason he was no longer in the mood to dally. After he settled things with Miller—really, there were many experienced women who were more than willing to slip away for a quick tumble—then he could put thoughts of Iris behind him.

The widow finally slunk away, annoyance clear

in her sullen expression and in the way she straightened her shoulders as she turned to leave.

He moved into the shadows and waited for Miller to arrive. Hopefully Iris wouldn't run into him first. He very much wanted to have a *talk* with the man.

CHAPTER 2

Wentworth was jolted back to the present when the carriage slowed to a halt. He'd gone over that scene far too often in the past six months, allowing that brief encounter with Iris Rowland to take up too much of his thoughts.

That would change today. He would come to his senses when he saw her again and realized she was far too young and inexperienced for him. That he'd allowed some hitherto unknown sense of sentimentality to take hold.

He'd be on his way back to London tomorrow morning and would resume his normal life, unfettered by concerns for the young woman he'd saved from certain ruin.

A footman opened the carriage door, allowing cold air into the warm interior of the carriage. He stepped down, making a mental note to see that the driver was rewarded handsomely.

He glanced up at the clouds above as he crossed the short distance to the front door and couldn't help but wonder if they were a sign snow was on the way. He pushed aside the grim thought of being trapped here for days and kept moving forward.

The butler swung the door open before he could raise a hand, and he was greeted by a small welcoming party. The dowager viscountess and Lady Thornton smiled in greeting and curtsied. Behind the two women, standing like vigilant sentries, were the two obstacles he'd have to overcome. Viscount Thornton and the Earl of Seaford.

Satisfaction swept through him at Seaford's presence. If he was there, then it was likely his sister-in-law, Iris, would be also.

Lady Thornton was the first to speak. "We are so happy to have you here. But I must admit it came as something of a surprise to see your name on the guest list. It was my understanding that you didn't like house parties."

It seemed that Thornton's wife had a backbone. Wentworth could respect that.

He bowed over her hand and smiled, doing his best to call forth all the charm for which he was famous. "I've heard so many wonderful things about your yearly Christmas gathering and sought an invitation. I am so pleased you were able to accommodate me."

Lady Thornton nodded in reply, but he could tell she was doubtful about his presence. Her mother-in-law, however, was beaming.

The dowager offered her hand, and he bowed over it as well. "Thank you for interceding on my behalf."

She gave him an arch look that spoke volumes. She'd issued the invitation, yes, but she was curious about his presence. It appeared his excuse hadn't fooled anyone. "If you'd like to get settled, I can have a footman show you to your room."

And that's when the two men stepped forward and Thornton spoke. "If you don't mind, we'd like to speak with you privately first."

Thornton shared a significant look with his wife, and Wentworth knew what was coming. The viscount was going to warn him about proper behavior.

He shot an amused glance at Seaford. Before last year, when the man had courted Miss Lily

Rowland, Seaford's reputation had been as wild as his own. It seemed a little hypocritical for Seaford to be a part of this conversation.

But Wentworth refused to let their presence deter him. After all, he would only be here for one day at most.

❄

WENTWORTH WASN'T SURPRISED WHEN THE TWO MEN led him to Thornton's study and closed the door.

"I must say, I'm honored to be singled out for such an auspicious welcome. Or is this your customary greeting?"

Seaford's lips twitched, but then he gained control of his features. Thornton's expression of course turned even grimmer. It appeared that marriage had cost the man his sense of humor.

Thornton folded his arms across his chest. "Why are you here?"

Wentworth raised a brow. "I received a gracious invitation from your mother, the dowager viscountess."

Thornton made a scoffing sound. "You went out of your way to obtain that invitation. For the life of me, I don't know why she agreed to have you here."

He shrugged. There was no point denying it. He'd had to call in several favors.

"Who are you pursuing?" Seaford was leaning against the desk, his body more at ease. He wasn't scowling like Thornton, but Wentworth suspected that would change once he learned the truth.

"Come on, man," Thornton said. "We all know you didn't accept an invitation to a country house party because you were feeling lonely and wanted to celebrate the festive season with us."

It seemed Thornton was going to be a thorn in his side. His lips quirked at the pun, but he thought it best not to laugh aloud.

He glanced at Seaford again. The earl had once been considered a rake, so he knew he didn't have any prudish sensibilities. But after marrying Iris's sister last Christmas, he seemed to have settled down.

He realized that the same could be said of him after he'd met Iris. He hadn't had one lover in that time, which was an intolerable situation. His mind shied away from thoughts that he might be ready to settle down himself.

But there was something about Iris that had intrigued him.

"I find it interesting that you had no problem welcoming Seaford into your extended family and into your home. Did he get the same inquisition about his intentions?"

Seaford barked out a laugh. "The ass actually warned Lily's family about me. Told them I couldn't be trusted."

Thornton shrugged. "It was the truth."

"And yet here you are, joining Thornton in questioning me about my motives."

Seaford aimed a scowl at the viscount. "Yes. Despite Thornton's sabotage, I managed to prevail."

Thornton merely shrugged. "He was sniffing around after my wife's cousin."

"I can understand your caution, but it's unwarranted. Have you ever heard anyone accuse me of taking advantage of a woman?"

Seaford shook his head. "If you have nothing to hide, then you can tell us why you're here."

Wentworth let out a loud breath as he gave up all pretense. Everyone was going to realize why he was here the moment he spoke to Iris. He met

Seaford's gaze and braced for whatever might come. "Your wife's middle sister."

Seaford actually paled. "Iris? Devil take it, Lily is going to kill me if we don't turn you out right now."

Wentworth raised one shoulder. "I wouldn't worry too much about it. I don't expect I'll be here long."

Seaford's entire demeanor changed. He rose to his feet and took a menacing step closer. "If you're thinking about defiling her and leaving, I'm going to have to call you out right now."

Wentworth held up his hands. "No, stop. That came out all wrong. But the damned woman has been in my thoughts since the season ended, and I need to exorcise her." He shook his head, hating that he had to explain himself to these two men, but he couldn't be turned out before seeing this thing through. "I'm sure a conversation or two will be enough to show me she's just another silly and frivolous young woman. I just caught her in a serious moment. After speaking to her again, I'll be able to set aside my curiosity about her."

Thornton actually laughed. "Clearly you don't know Iris if that's what you think."

Seaford shook his head. "Iris might be young,

but she has a level head on her shoulders. All the Rowland women do. It's unsettling."

Wentworth frowned, pushing back the doubt that was beginning to creep in. He'd already started on this course of action and must continue. "Duly noted. Am I allowed to leave this room now?"

Thornton let out a resigned sigh. "Just know that we're watching you."

Wentworth inclined his head, accepting the inevitable scrutiny. He would expect nothing less and would deal with their overprotective behavior for his short stay.

CHAPTER 3

Iris left her bedchamber and made her way downstairs.

She was always late getting started whenever she had to travel. The trip to her cousin Celia's home wasn't a long one, so the carriage ride hadn't been overly strenuous. But she hadn't been able to sleep last night because of her excitement.

She wandered down to the drawing room, where she could hear voices floating out into the hall. She hesitated a moment outside, listening to the excited murmurs. She caught giggles and only snippets of whispers. *Can't believe he's here… He never attends house parties… Do you think he's planning on settling down…*

The speculation sparked her curiosity. Hoping

to find someone she knew, she stepped into the room.

The space was filled with many of the female guests who were clustered together on the settee or standing in groups. They all seemed to be talking about this mysterious guest.

Iris's curiosity was engaged. Her thoughts immediately flew to the man she'd met near the end of the season in London. Lord Wentworth. His arrival at such an event would surely spark this level of speculation among all the women, both young and old. But Wentworth would never attend a Christmas house party in the country.

From everything she'd heard about the man, he was a confirmed rakehell. And the way he'd gone from complimenting her to heading off with a buxom woman into the bowels of the garden, a wicked smirk on her face, had set her blood boiling.

No, he would never attend such an event, which was exactly to her liking because she never wanted to see him again.

Her eyes swept over the room and settled on the two women she wanted to see, who were clustered by the window. Her sister Lily and her cousin Celia.

They met her gaze, and she smiled in greeting, but before she took even one step in their direction, the air in the room changed abruptly. Whispers were silenced, and everyone turned to look at her.

She took in their wide eyes and gaping expressions. A few quickly covered their surprise, while others continued to stare at her avidly as though they'd never seen her before.

She looked down at her dress, wondering if something was amiss, but could see nothing wrong. Then she lifted a hand to her hair. She'd pinned it up carefully after waking from her nap. Had it come loose?

"I think they're staring at me. You, as always, are impeccable and lovely."

She froze, shock washing over her at the voice coming from over her left shoulder. No, she was imagining things.

Slowly, half expecting to discover that she was still in bed and was, in fact, dreaming, she shifted to the left and met Lord Wentworth's amused expression.

"I'm dreaming." Her voice was barely above a whisper. Would she even remember this when she woke up? She rarely remembered her dreams. How often had Wentworth invaded her thoughts while she was sleeping?

One corner of his mouth quirked up into that smirk that had so unsettled her when they met.

"I can't fault you for thinking so, but I am very real."

She was about to reach out and pinch him but in the end decided it would be best to pinch her own arm. With all the eyes on them now, it wouldn't do to be caught touching the man in the unlikely event this was actually happening.

She squeezed her fingers together over the skin of her forearm and twisted, then winced at the spark of pain.

His eyes narrowed on the movement, his forehead now creased in a frown. For one absurd moment, she thought he was going to reach out to soothe the small hurt she'd given herself.

"My lord, how nice of you to join us," Celia said, appearing on her right.

Her sister Lily appeared on her left. "If you're looking for the gentlemen, I believe they're in the billiard room."

His forehead cleared, and his expression took on his customary amusement. As though there was a running dialogue inside his head and he was constantly coming up with funny witticisms to explain what was happening around him. She wondered what that voice was saying about this current turn of events.

No. She couldn't allow herself to wonder anything about this man. He was an experienced man of the world. A rake. He wasn't interested in her at all, not when he spent his free time gambling with his peers and bedding loose women.

Her stomach soured at the thought of the other women he'd been with, but she refused to allow him to see it. He met her gaze, and she got the impression that he wanted to speak to *her*. In private.

"Of course," he said. "I didn't realize that we were segregating our activities based on sex." The way he emphasized that last word, as though he were intentionally trying to shock them, had her interest sparking anew. Damn this man. Why was he so captivating?

Celia and Lily shifted closer to her, and she realized they were trying to protect her. She wanted to laugh at them. Lord Wentworth was most definitely *not* interested in her, much to her chagrin.

The dowager viscountess swept into the room then, and the expression on her face was almost comical. It was inconceivable to her that he would have stumbled into the drawing room when it was clearly set aside for just the women right then.

Clearly she knew nothing about the man's reputation. Iris had only met the man once, but she would have guessed that if one were in search of Wentworth, they should look to where the women were congregating.

Or secreted away in one of the bedchambers with someone. Somehow she kept her mouth from twisting at that thought.

They moved to the side as Celia's mother-in-law placed herself squarely before him, for all intents and purposes as though she were guarding the entrance.

"My lord, I understand that this is your first house party. There will be ample opportunity for everyone to gather together later. But we've learned over the years that men like their time alone together."

Wentworth met her gaze again over the dowager's shoulder, and she came to a bizarre realization that she could read his thoughts. And Wentworth wanted her to know that what the dowager viscountess was saying was that it was the women who wanted some time away from the men so that they could gossip.

And since they'd been doing just that when she arrived, she couldn't deny it. She lifted one shoulder in a small shrug, and his eyes sparked with amusement.

He turned back to Lady Thornton. "Of course. I must have gotten the hours wrong. I thought we were to all meet here."

"Oh no, there is a set time when the men can gather together in various areas of the house. I'll make sure that someone gives the schedule to your valet. Until then…"

Iris wanted to stay and hear what he was going to say next. Or barring that, stay and see if she could read his thoughts again the next time he looked at her. But while the dowager viscountess droned on about the schedule, Celia and Lily linked their arms through hers and took her back to the spot they'd commandeered near the window.

It took every ounce of strength she had not to glance back to see what was happening in the doorway. "Is Violet still in her room? And I don't see Clara."

Lily gave her head a small shake. "Violet wanted to write a letter to a friend. Honestly, she's always writing letters of late. I'm a little worried about her. Will she even know how to engage with people next season when she comes out? At least

Seaford's sister is often with her, so she isn't completely feral."

Iris laughed. "I know you're not able to visit as often now that you're married, but I can assure you that our sister doesn't spend all her time writing letters." She waited until Lily let out a small sigh of relief before adding, "At least not when she's visiting with Clara. Otherwise, she spends the rest of her time reading."

Lily grimaced, and Iris couldn't hold back her laugh. Violet had always enjoyed reading and scribbling in her journal. To be honest, Iris had been relieved when their youngest sister had started writing letters to various acquaintances.

Celia leaned in close, her voice barely above a whisper. "You need to take care, Iris. My husband told me that Lord Wentworth has accepted this invitation because of you."

Iris couldn't help it, she burst out laughing at the earnest expression on her cousin's face.

"This is quite serious. You need to be careful and make sure you're never alone with him."

"Well, perhaps that's going a bit too far," Lily added. "I'm sure a minute here or there throughout the next few days won't cause a scandal. Everyone else will be doing it. Besides, if he's decided to court my sister, we need to give him the opportunity to do so."

Iris looked from her sister, who seemed to believe what she was saying, to Celia, whose mouth had set into a disapproving line. Surely they didn't believe the fiction they were telling her.

"I think Thornton is having fun at your expense," she said, trying to ease her cousin's very obvious distress. "Lord Wentworth is someone who enjoys spending time with experienced women. There is nothing you can say to make me believe that he came here to see *me*." She let out another laugh, but this one had an edge to it she didn't want to think about. Disappointment, perhaps?

"I think Celia is correct. Simon told me the same thing, and he wanted me to keep an eye on you."

She pierced her sister with a penetrating glance and was careful to keep her voice low when she replied to that ridiculous admonishment. "Would this be the same husband who kidnapped you and spent the night with you, *alone*, in a small cottage before you were married?"

Lily's eyes widened, and she glanced about them to see if anyone had overheard. When she was satisfied no one was near, she hissed back at her, "Are you trying to cause a scandal?"

"No, I'm just trying to point out that you married a rake, and he changed his ways. It's possible that Lord Wentworth might be trying to do the same."

"Simon courted me for months, and he was a perfect gentleman during that period. He only…" She waved her hand, unwilling to repeat Iris's words lest they be overheard. "I'd turned down his proposal of marriage because I thought he only wanted me because I would make a convenient bride."

"Yes, yes, but instead, he's wildly passionate about you." Honestly, was it necessary for her sister to rub in the fact that she'd found happiness when Iris's own season had ended in disappointment?

Celia covered her mouth to hide her snort of laughter.

Lily rolled her eyes. "You don't have room to criticize me. Thornton is equally devoted to you."

The two smiled at one another, and Iris rolled her eyes. "I'm going to go check on Violet and try to coax her to join us. The two of you can continue to congratulate yourselves on having secured love matches while I'm gone."

She began to turn, but Lily stopped her and whispered into her ear, "Promise me you'll act with caution."

"Of course," Iris said with a nod. It was an easy promise to make since she knew she was in no danger from Wentworth.

CHAPTER 4

The afternoon had passed by pleasantly enough, filled mainly with several rounds of billiards and various card games. They'd played only for bragging rights, something he hadn't done since he was a youth. But it seemed that it was equally enjoyable to win even if there wasn't money involved… and he'd won far more than he'd lost.

It got tiring after a while having to play off the curious glances and outright questions from everyone about why he was there. If these people could accept a rake like Seaford into their midst, then he couldn't understand why they were so surprised that he'd be in attendance.

It was an effort not to dwell on his all-too-brief

interaction with Iris Rowland several hours earlier. A sense of unease had settled over him after being unceremoniously led away from the drawing room by Thornton's mother.

She'd said all the right things, of course, but it was clear that something had changed with respect to how she viewed him. He'd had to call in several favors among friends of the family to get this invitation, but the woman's welcome when he first arrived was a far cry from her demeanor when she'd come across him performing the unspeakable act of trying to enter the drawing room.

Iris had been right there, but it was now clear that the world was conspiring against him.

He rolled his shoulders as he waited for Iris to leave her bedchamber. His valet had learned where Iris was sleeping, but he wasn't such a brute as to storm into her room. Instead, he'd found a discrete alcove to lurk in near the end of the hallway and lay in wait, very much like a villain in a horrid novel.

It was humbling to be the one doing the chasing. Not that he was chasing after Iris, of course. He just needed to speak to her so he could finally set aside the curiosity that had him obsessing about their meeting in the garden months ago.

He wasn't quite sure how he would accomplish

that during the evening's entertainments. The sanctioned mingling period between the sexes before dinner.

Fortunately, the wait wasn't a long one, so he wouldn't have to try to convince someone that he'd lost his way. The manor house was large, yes, but it was laid out in much the same manner as countless other houses he'd visited.

Iris exited her bedroom, and he was just about to approach her when she was followed by her younger sister as well as Seaford's sister.

He let out an amused huff at his own presumption that this would be easy. Nothing thus far had been. This was yet another roadblock he'd have to overcome.

They would have to pass by him before heading downstairs, so he waited for her to approach. He watched her smile at something her sister said. Then, sensing his presence, she turned her head toward him, her smile freezing in place.

She said something to her two companions and then headed toward him. The younger women waited, clearly curious about what was happening.

Iris stopped when she reached him and shook her head. Her expression was very much one of bemusement, as though she'd found him sneaking a treat before dinner.

"Why am I not surprised to find you lurking outside the bedrooms assigned to the female guests?"

He chuckled. "I see you haven't lost your wit."

She raised one shoulder. "If a man is scared away by a woman's intelligence, then he isn't worth knowing."

She folded her arms across her chest and waited for his response. He could tell that she was assessing his reaction to her statement. There was a resignation within that told him he'd already been judged and found wanting.

"I'm not afraid of a woman's intelligence."

She searched his face, no doubt looking for any clue that would tell her he was lying. He knew she'd find none. Others might prefer a woman who was simply a decorative accessory, but he liked his women with a little more substance.

"There are few men who would agree with you."

"That would be their failing."

They stared at one another for several seconds. Finally, she let out a soft huff of air.

"I don't know who is assigned to which room, so

it seems you'll have to wait a little longer to meet your paramour."

He knew she meant the words as a set down, but to him it felt like a challenge. If she thought he would be so easily dismissed, then he'd have to show her otherwise.

"There is no paramour in residence here, but"—he took a step closer and lowered his voice—"if you'd like to apply for the position, I'd be willing to consider your application."

Her eyes widened a fraction, and he waited for her reaction. He should have known that she'd surprise him yet again when she let out a hearty laugh. He couldn't help but join her, so infectious was her mirth.

Finally, her amusement faded, but her eyes were still twinkling. And she was actually smiling at him. "You are incorrigible. I can see why everyone has rushed to warn me about you."

He wasn't surprised at the knowledge. But at least her family hadn't seen fit to position a footman outside her bedroom door. Thank goodness for small mercies.

He smiled down at her. "But you're not afraid of me." It wasn't a question since it was clear Iris wasn't afraid for her virtue. Not at the moment.

She shook her head. "You had me alone in a dark garden. If you wanted to ravish me, you would have done it then."

She turned away and started back down the hallway. He fell into step beside her.

She glanced sideways at him. "Won't your paramour be disappointed if you abandon your wait so soon? I promise not to tell anyone."

He leaned closer and murmured, "I'm here for you, Iris Rowland."

Her steps faltered, but then she straightened and continued to her two companions.

"Allow me to introduce you, my lord, to my sister, Miss Violet Rowland, and to my good friend, Miss Clara Howe. This is Lord Wentworth."

He bowed his greeting to the two younger women. "It is a pleasure to meet the two of you."

Iris fell into step next to her two companions, and he trailed just behind them.

She glanced at him over her shoulders, and he could see her surprise that he was still with them. He grinned at her. She'd learn soon enough that he was only here for her.

Her lips tightened into a line before she turned away. She did lean slightly toward the other two and say, her voice clear, "He's something of a reprobate, so watch yourselves around him."

He let out a startled laugh. He'd been dreading this visit, thinking that he'd need to put it behind him quickly so that he could continue with his normal life, but after one short conversation with Iris, everything had changed. He'd have to inform his valet that they wouldn't be leaving tomorrow morning.

CHAPTER 5

Iris found it impossible to ignore Wentworth's presence. After their chance meeting that evening all those months ago, she'd never expected to speak to him again. Given the type of woman with whom he normally associated, she certainly never expected him to seek her out.

Which was why her gaze kept drifting over to him when he wasn't close by. She expected that a more sophisticated woman wouldn't be quite so obvious, but Iris wasn't up to that level of pretense. Wentworth had told her that he was here for her, but she couldn't allow herself to believe him.

She took note of who he was speaking to and expected him to slip away at some point. When that didn't happen before dinner, she told herself that he was being discreet for now and would slip away to meet someone after dinner when people had wandered off to experience one of the entertainments during the evening.

She hadn't expected him to be seated next to her during the meal and suspected that he must have switched out the name cards to achieve that outcome.

She concentrated on speaking to the older gentleman to her right and his wife, who was seated across from them. And she absolutely was not straining to hear what Wentworth was saying to the widow who was to his left. But every time he chuckled, the soft sound had her hackles rising.

Finally, during a lull in the conversation near the end of the main course, he leaned close to her.

"You've been uncharacteristically silent toward me. And after all the trouble I undertook to ensure we were seated next to one another."

Her eyes narrowed on him, and she couldn't help but wonder what game he was playing. Perhaps he was trying to make the widow jealous. For one moment she considered telling him not to bother trying to charm her, but she'd be lying to both of them. Even if he was using her as a pawn in another game, there was no reason she couldn't enjoy herself.

She lowered her voice and prayed no one could overhear their conversation. "If you need my assistance in trying to make someone else jealous, I'm willing to play along." Then she laughed softly and spoke in what she hoped was a normal tone. She'd never tried her hand at acting a role before today. "Pray continue. I'd love to hear the rest of that story."

He chuckled in reply, for all the world seeming as though she'd genuinely amused him. It was clear he was far more skilled at pretense than she.

"I'll win you over yet, Miss Rowland."

He'd tire of this game soon enough, but for now she was willing to accept his attention. It wasn't as though anyone else was trying to capture her interest. Wentworth was the only single gentleman under the age of fifty in attendance.

Now that Iris wasn't intent on ignoring the man while simultaneously trying to overhear what he was saying to his other dinner companion, the rest of the meal passed far more pleasantly. She was included in his conversation with the widow, and the situation baffled her. It seemed that the woman was already engaged to another. Iris looked for clues to any hidden meaning behind their words but she couldn't detect a hint of romance between the two.

After the meal was over, the men remained in the dining room to enjoy their port and to smoke. She imagined that she could feel Wentworth's eyes on her as she left with the rest of the women. She couldn't resist turning back to look at him when she was in the doorway and was shocked to discover it hadn't been her imagination.

The men were all standing, of course, but he was the only one who hadn't already turned to engage in conversation with another. His head tilted to one side, and she could tell he'd been waiting for her to look back at him.

She shrugged in reply. She was a novice at whatever game he was playing, so of course he would have the upper hand.

When they reached the ballroom, which had been turned into a salon for the house party, she was surrounded yet again by her older sister and her cousin. They drew her a little way down the hall and waited for the other women to enter the ballroom before turning to face her.

Celia's brows were drawn together. "I was very careful with the seating plan to ensure that you weren't seated next to Lord Wentworth."

A small zing went through her at that piece of information. He hadn't been lying about that after all. She'd wanted to believe him but wasn't sure it was prudent to take anything he said at face value.

Lily didn't bother to hide her amusement. "Clearly he had someone switch the place cards."

Iris smiled. "Is that why you had them this year? Thornton's mother usually allowed people to sit where they wanted when she was hosting the parties."

Celia let out a soft sigh. "They were a last-minute addition. I was trying to avoid this very thing, but it appears I shouldn't have bothered."

Lily bumped shoulders with Celia. "I'm sure it will be fine. There was no harm done."

"Says the woman who married a reformed rake." Celia turned to Iris. "You might not be so fortunate, Iris. I don't know why he seems to be fixated on you, but you should be careful."

Her cousin's warning had the exact opposite effect on her. Iris would need to be careful lest she betray the fact that she was actually enjoying the man's attention.

She tried to keep her tone light lest she betray that fact. "He seems well-liked, even among the men. Surely he isn't such a blackguard."

"That's the way of it with men," Lily said. "I've seen it often enough with my own husband. Every man wants to be their friend, and every woman wants to bed them."

Iris stared at her sister in shock. "Still? Even though he's clearly devoted to you?" A horrible thought occurred to her. "Surely he doesn't *entertain* these other women."

"Oh no," Lily said. "I have no fears in that department. But it can be unsettling watching another woman try to lure him from my side. Many aren't even subtle about it."

Celia let out a soft laugh. "But it's very amusing to watch their annoyance when our husbands turn them away."

"So how can you be sure that a man's interest is genuine?"

Celia and Lily shared a look before her cousin spoke. "You can't, not really. You just have to listen to your heart *and* your head. Many a young woman has allowed herself to be carried away by thoughts of fairy-tale endings. But they ignore the warning signs."

Iris nodded, taking in the wisdom of those words even while she longed to give in to the romance of having a charismatic man pursue her.

"So I need to watch how he behaves with the other women." She turned to Celia. "Was everyone present at dinner?"

"Yes. Why do you ask?"

"I was just wondering if perhaps his paramour was here. But since he was sitting next to me, she might not have come down for dinner."

Celia shook her head. "Everyone was here. Perhaps that's why he's fixed his attention on you. He might see you as a likely target, someone who is easy to manipulate."

Iris wanted to leap to Wentworth's defense, but she couldn't allow her cousin to know that she was thinking about entertaining his pursuit to see where it ended.

Instead, she shared the small piece of information she'd been keeping to herself. "We met in London. Near the end of the season."

Lily's hand flew to her mouth, and Celia became unnaturally still. It was hard not to squirm under their twin stares.

Her sister reached for her hand. "You didn't tell me. Did he… Surely he didn't proposition you?" The words were said in a harsh whisper.

She really didn't want to share her foolish misstep, but she had to let Celia and Lily know that Wentworth wasn't a complete blackguard. "No, he was a gentleman. But he did find me alone."

Lily's eyes narrowed. "When did this happen?"

"During a ball. I slipped out into the gardens to meet someone."

Celia clutched her arm. "Wentworth?"

She shook her head. "Someone else. It doesn't matter who. Wentworth saw me, we spoke for a little while, and he convinced me to return inside. Apparently the person I was going to meet had just offered for someone else, so his intentions weren't honorable."

Celia let out a breath. "So Wentworth didn't take advantage of you. And it sounds like he might have stopped someone else from doing just that."

Lily nudged her again. "I told you. Not all rakes are out to ruin the innocence of every young maiden they happen upon."

"Perhaps not. But he's here now, and he's made his interest in you clear."

Iris lifted one shoulder, feigning a nonchalance she was far from feeling. "He's just passing the time."

"He wasn't on the original guest list. Thornton's mother added him at the last minute, and she didn't tell me or her son until after the invitation had gone out."

Lily's eyes were gleaming with interest now. "Why would she do that?"

Her cousin's eyes remained fixed on Iris. "She was approached by someone and asked to invite him. She wouldn't say who that person was, but apparently Wentworth was very eager to be here."

Iris's heart was starting to race. "He was speaking to another female guest during the meal."

Celia shook her head. "No, this person asked whether the Rowland sisters would be in attendance. After my mother-in-law told them that you'd all been invited, they told her that Lord Wentworth would consider himself beholden to the family if he received an invitation."

Lily's eyes were wide now with the same excitement Iris was trying to tamp down within herself. "Do you think he wants to court you?"

Iris wanted to believe that. But despite everything she'd heard today, both now and from Wentworth himself, she still needed to guard her heart. She kept replaying the way that meeting in the garden had ended, with the man admonishing her to go back inside.

But she'd hurried past another woman who was

walking down that darkened garden path. Someone older and more worldly. Iris had watched from the shadows as that woman threw herself into Wentworth's arms before she'd turned and fled. She hadn't wanted to see what the two of them would do next.

No, she couldn't compete with the type of women that normally interested this man. She couldn't allow herself to fall into the romantic notion that she would be able to reform a rake, the way Lily had.

She would try to enjoy herself during this house party, and if that meant witty conversations with Wentworth, she'd throw herself wholeheartedly into the pastime. But she needed to be careful to guard her heart in the process.

CHAPTER 6

Finally, the men finished their drinks, and they made their way to the ballroom to join the women. Wentworth had no qualms about disappointing the few older gentlemen who wanted to return to the billiard room for the rest of the evening. He was there for only one person. Iris.

The ballroom had been turned into a salon for the house party. Small seating arrangements were scattered throughout the space, and there were card tables set up for those who wanted to play whist. Evergreen boughs and festive decorations were hung on the walls and scattered throughout the room. Off to one side, there was a long table laden with refreshments, and someone was playing soft music on a pianoforte.

The effect was warm and charming, but his gaze settled immediately on Iris. She was sitting on a settee on the far side of the room, flanked by both her older sister and cousin. Seaford's wife nudged Iris's shoulder and whispered something in her ear.

For a moment he feared she was telling Iris that she wouldn't be leaving her side. Relief filled him several seconds later when the countess rose to greet her husband. Lady Thornton also rose to greet her own husband. Which left Iris unguarded.

Or at least as much as one could be in a room filled with far too many people.

Iris smiled at him then, which was all the encouragement he needed. Never one to miss an opportunity, he crossed the room and settled next to her.

"I wonder how long we'll be able to speak together before someone comes to whisk you away."

Iris tilted her head to one side, her blue eyes crinkling with amusement. "I think it far more likely that you'll grow bored with me and seek out another."

"And how would that make you feel?"

His eyes remained fixed on hers as she considered the question. Another woman would be coy, making an exaggerated comment about how all her hopes and dreams would be dashed. Or they'd pretend indifference. Of course Iris would be different.

"Honestly? I'm not sure how I would feel."

"I would hope you'd be disappointed. I know I would be."

She examined him, and he waited, hoping she'd be able to tell he spoke the truth.

Finally, she nodded. "I don't understand why you're here." She lowered her voice before continuing. "I've been told that you sought this invitation because you wanted to see me again."

"I did."

Had he ever felt this vulnerable with a woman? Not since his first experience bedding an older widow who was very eager to mold him into the perfect lover. But back then he'd been concerned about his lack of experience hampering his performance. Right now he was worried about this woman, who was barely out of the schoolroom, finding him wanting as a person. And for the life of him, he couldn't understand why.

She nodded, accepting his admission. "Why?"

When he'd set out to secure an invitation to the annual Thornton Christmas house party, he hadn't expected to be on the receiving end of Iris's questions.

"Honestly? I don't know why. But I've been thinking about that meeting, and I needed to see you again."

She let out a soft sigh and glanced away. "Of course. You wanted to make sure that I hadn't continued with my foolish quest to find love with unworthy men who just wanted to take advantage of me."

His chest constricted as he remembered how close that had come to happening. He wanted to reach for her but couldn't, not with so many people surrounding them. But blessedly, they'd been provided with a measure of solitude for now.

It seemed they were being aided by Thornton and Seaford and their wives. They were standing nearby, chatting together. Close enough that he and Iris weren't truly alone, but they did waylay anyone who was heading in their direction by engaging them in conversation or mentioning how good the wassail was this year.

"Iris." He waited until she turned to meet his gaze. "I will forever be grateful that I found you out in the garden that evening. But I am not here as someone who is checking on your well-being."

She licked her lips, and he wanted to groan. "Then why are you here?"

He'd come this far, but instead of being convinced his interest in this young woman was nothing but a foolish whim, he was beginning to think it went deeper. "I'm here because I can't stop thinking about you."

She shook her head but said nothing.

She didn't believe him. He wanted to laugh aloud at the absurd thought. Of course she didn't. She had to have known that he was out in that garden because he too was planning to meet someone. She might not have known his reputation then, but she would have been enlightened about his character once he made his interest in her known to Thornton and Seaford.

And dammit, he admired her for it. Because now he knew that she wasn't a silly creature given to flights of fancy. She wouldn't just take his word for it that something deeper had happened between them out in that garden.

That he was here because he'd become obsessed with her. He who'd never been captivated by another woman couldn't stop thinking about this one. And coming here to speak with her again had only cemented his interest.

Violet Rowland dropped onto the settee next to her sister, ending their brief moment of privacy. She twined her arm through her sister's. "We're going to sing Christmas carols soon."

Iris smiled at her sister. "I'll join you in a minute."

Violet turned to give him an assessing look. Her eyes were a lighter shade of blue, but there could be no doubt that they were siblings. "Do you sing, my lord?"

He chuckled. "Rest assured, you do *not* want to hear me sing."

Violet took him at his word and went to join the small group that was gathering by the pianoforte.

Iris gave him an arch look. "Perhaps you should have some wassail to ease your fears of performing."

"There are many things at which I excel. Singing is not one of them."

Instead of pouting, she shrugged. "I should go."

He was surprised at the reluctance he felt at the idea of Iris leaving his side. "Will you join me again after?"

She considered the request. "I can't ignore everyone else. If you'd like to speak privately, you should know that I like to break my fast early. It's usually fairly quiet in the breakfast room at that hour."

He nodded and watched her go. At least he'd be able to continue watching her as she sang. And he'd be able to speak to her tomorrow morning.

CHAPTER 7

Nothing would have prevented him from waking early and heading down to the breakfast room.

Iris had been correct—there were only a few people at that hour. Fortunately, he wouldn't have to wait to speak to her again. She was already seated at the table, along with her younger sister and Seaford's sister.

"Good morning," he said as he passed them on the way to the sideboard.

He could feel Iris's eyes on him, but he didn't turn around. And the trio's voices had lowered. He hoped that was because they were talking about him.

Iris wasn't sitting in the middle, thank goodness,

and the seat next to her was still empty when he returned with his filled plate to the table. He would take that as a good sign.

"You're up early, my lord. I would have thought you'd be the sort to lie abed until midday."

He took a sip of tea and met her eyes. Their gazes held for several seconds. He waged and lost an internal battle to combat his worst impulses. "Do you often imagine me in bed?"

Her eyes widened a fraction at his outrageous taunt, but in the end, she merely shook her head in exasperation. "I'll concede the point in this match to you."

He behaved himself for the rest of the meal. A few people wandered in but, fortunately, none of the people who had appointed themselves to making sure he behaved himself.

"So what are you planning to do this morning, my lord?" she said when she'd finished.

Violet and Clara had already wandered off, and for the moment, they were the only guests still seated. The footmen were refilling some of the trays, and he knew that others would be arriving.

"I'm not sure. What does one do so early at such an event when many of the guests are still sleeping? I'll admit I've never been on this side of such a situation before."

She laughed. "We entertain ourselves. I was heading to the library to find something to read."

She stood, and he did as well. "That sounds acceptable. Perhaps you can show me the way? In case I'm ever in need of reading material, of course."

"Of course," she said.

He saw the ghost of something flitter across her face, but she masked it quickly. They exited the breakfast room, and he fell into step beside her.

"The library is on the second floor. It is quite large. You'll have to tell me how it compares to yours." She stopped and turned to look at him. "You do have a library?"

Did she think him a barbarian who didn't read? "Of course. Several, in fact. I'm sure you would enjoy exploring all the nooks and crannies of the various libraries in my holdings."

He froze as soon as the words left his mouth. No woman who wasn't already a member of his family had visited any of his estates. Not even his town house in London. He liked to conduct his affairs away from his residences. So much easier to slip away when it was time to go.

If Iris thought his words strange, she didn't show it. And honestly, he was overreacting. It was an innocent statement. He was tying himself in knots over this young woman, and he didn't know why.

They said nothing further as they made their way upstairs. Fortunately, they only ran into two footmen along the way. The men didn't even glance their way. Thornton was a fool. His host should have assigned a footman to follow along behind him to ensure he behaved. Wentworth would never be so trusting.

They arrived at the room in question. It was large but nothing out of the ordinary. It certainly wouldn't compare with the library at his country seat.

He followed her into the room, and she didn't protest.

They were well away from the door when she slipped behind a bookshelf that divided the room. Curious, he followed.

He wasn't sure what he expected, probably that she was scampering up one of the ladders to reach a book on a high shelf. Instead, she was facing him, arms crossed.

He stopped opposite her and waited.

She licked her lower lip, and he was powerless to stop his gaze from settling briefly on her mouth. He'd wondered, of course, what it would be like to kiss Iris. He didn't actually believe he'd get that opportunity.

"I would like you to kiss me," she said.

It took him a moment to realize she'd actually spoken aloud and that his mind hadn't conjured this moment out of his frustrations. He hesitated another moment as he considered asking her whether he'd heard her correctly, but he hated that it would make him appear the callow youth.

He compromised by closing the space between them, making sure to move slowly so that she had ample opportunity to put a stop to what was about to happen. Because one thing was certain. If Iris wanted him to kiss her, he most definitely wasn't going to convince her that it wasn't a wise idea.

He was still operating under the assumption that his fixation on this woman rested in the unknown. Spending time in her presence hadn't convinced him that she was just like many other women. To the contrary, his curiosity about her had only increased.

But his recent attempts to forget her with other women had led to an ennui with the fairer sex that had frustrated him. Kissing Iris Rowland might end similarly—with him feeling a cold indifference.

He stopped when mere inches separated them. She tilted her face up to him, and he couldn't deny that a powerful sense of anticipation was already thrumming through his veins.

He reached for her chin at the same moment she placed her palms on his chest and leaned into him. She was shorter than him, and he bent to kiss her.

The first touch of his mouth on hers was light, so the zing that sped through him was unexpected. Her soft sigh followed by a small sound at the back of her throat set fire to his senses. He was powerless to stop himself from dragging her fully into his arms, but she came willingly, her arms wrapping around his neck as though she wanted to keep him with her forever.

Their kiss deepened, tongues warring with one another. Her movements were awkward at first, making it clear that she'd never kissed anyone before. He'd wondered, of course, if there had been any other men after he'd thwarted her meeting with Miller. It would be the height of hypocrisy to ask her, nor would he censure her if there had been another. But one thing was clear,

Iris hadn't expected to enjoy their embrace quite so much.

He forced himself to break the kiss, but he couldn't let her go. He gazed down at her upturned face. Her eyes were closed, her cheeks flushed, and a sense of possessiveness swept through him. He'd never felt this way before.

Shaken, he continued to stare at Iris as her mouth curled into a satisfied smile. Her eyes were unfocused when she finally opened them, and he swore he could see daydreams and fantasies flittering behind them.

"I'm no hero," he said, surprised at the rough timbre of his voice after only one kiss.

Her eyes sharpened, and they seemed to pierce through him as she studied his expression. Finally, she pulled away, and he dropped his arms with great reluctance.

"No, of course not. I would never confuse you for the hero of a fairy tale. So if that's what you're thinking, you can rest easy knowing that I have no illusions about you."

Her statement shouldn't have surprised him, and he had to laugh at himself. Did he really think he could fell this woman with just one kiss?

He locked his hands behind his back so he

wouldn't drag her into his arms again. Because in that moment, he wanted nothing more than to do just that.

"Did anything precipitate this request?"

She looked away, and he didn't think she was going to reply. Finally, she sighed and clasped her hands at her waist. He wanted to believe it was to keep from reaching for him again.

"Last night, after retiring, I had difficulty falling asleep."

They had that in common. Thoughts of going to Iris's room had plagued him for hours. "Thinking of me?"

Her exasperated sigh had him wanting to laugh. "Not at first, no. I was thinking of my brother-in-law. And Celia's husband."

He frowned. That was not what he wanted to hear. "What about them?"

"Watching the way they behaved with their wives. The two of them were so devoted. And the way they would hold hands, stand a little too close…"

Yes, he'd seen it as well. "They couldn't wait for the evening to end so they could make love."

Heat rose to her cheeks. "And then there was you."

He stilled, forcing himself to wait for her to continue. He couldn't risk scaring her away, not when they might not have another moment alone. It was a miracle someone hadn't already walked into the library.

"I find it difficult to believe you're here because you wanted to see me again."

He shouldn't be surprised she still had doubts. "I did."

She was examining him closely, weighing the truth of his words. "I thought Celia and Lily were daft for even thinking such a thing was possible, but then…"

Unable to hold back any longer, he reached for one of her hands and brought it up to his mouth. "But then…?" he prompted with a kiss to her palm.

"I saw that same look on your face whenever I glanced your way."

One corner of his mouth lifted into a satisfied smile. He enjoyed the way her eyes narrowed in response. "I've always found that the best way to let someone know you're thinking about them isn't to ignore them."

"And no doubt you've had plenty of experience when it comes to pursuing women."

She tugged at her hand, but he didn't release

it. Couldn't release it. Her words bothered him more than they should. Not because they weren't true—all the ton knew that they were. But because she thought that she was just one of many when she stood far above any woman he'd ever been with.

A slight frown creased her brow, but she stilled and waited for him to speak.

"You are not just another woman I'm pursuing."

She let out a soft laugh, and this time when she tugged at her hand, he released it. "I'm sure you've told every woman you've been with the same thing."

"No, Iris. I've never uttered those words."

She lifted one shoulder. "Perhaps not those words exactly—"

"No."

"But in some other way, you've made them feel special, as though you saw only them."

She was starting to turn away. He reached for her and she stopped. Several seconds of tense silence passed, and then she lifted her gaze to his again.

He didn't release her. He liked the feel of his hand on her waist, and she didn't press the matter.

From the way her pupils had dilated, he knew that she liked it as well.

"I've never said anything remotely similar to another woman. And I was careful to avoid anyone who might want more than a casual encounter."

That crease between her brows was back again. "But I want to marry one day. I want what Lily and Celia have."

"Yes, I know. Which is why I tried to forget you after that encounter."

She looked away. "I passed that woman on the path, the one you were meeting. And I stopped to see what would happen. I saw the way she threw herself into your arms."

Her voice was small, and he hated hearing it, hated seeing the way she was drawing in on herself. As if she was doubting that she'd ever be able to hold his attention.

Before that meeting, he would have said she was correct.

"But you didn't stay."

She shook her head. "I'd seen enough. I had no desire to witness whatever was going to happen next."

He caressed her chin with the thumb of his other hand, watching the way she shivered at his touch. He had no intention of allowing Iris to leave until they'd finished this conversation.

"Look at me."

She closed her eyes for a brief moment, then straightened to her full height and turned to look at him. He was cupping her chin now.

"I pried her away from me and sent her home. Alone."

Her eyes widened. "I don't understand. You were there to meet with her."

"Yes, but then I ran across another woman who was on the verge of making the biggest mistake of her life."

She grasped his wrist but didn't pull his hand away. "I don't understand. I was already gone. I offered no impediment to your tryst."

"No, but you were in my thoughts. I couldn't be with that woman when all I wanted to do was chase after you and drag you back into the gardens with me."

He held her stare, willing her to see the truth of his words. "I tried to forget you, but it seems that I don't want anyone but you."

She didn't take that as a compliment, proving once again that Iris was wise beyond her years. "For how long, my lord? Surely not forever."

He winced at the accusation. She was right to doubt him, especially since he hadn't come here to offer her that which she clearly wanted. "I'm going to be honest with you, Iris. If we're to have anything, you need to know what I'm feeling."

She licked her lips. "And what is that?"

He barked out a laugh. "I'm damned confused. I've never felt this way before."

"Never?"

"No."

A smile broke out over her face, and his suddenly foolish heart lightened at the sight.

"Then perhaps we should explore this new emotion."

He had both hands on her waist now and was drawing her closer. "That might not be wise."

"Perhaps not, but it will be so much fun." And then she leaned into him again and raised her face for another kiss.

CHAPTER 8

To Iris's dismay, Wentworth pulled out of their embrace far too soon. He released her and took a step back.

He ran a hand through his hair. "I am trying to remember that I need to be on my best behavior, but you are making it deuced difficult."

It wasn't wise, but she liked the fact that he seemed so confused. "And if I don't want you to be a gentleman?"

Now he had both hands in his hair as he spun away from her. Somehow she resisted the urge to throw herself into his arms as she waited for his response.

Finally, he dropped his arms, straightened, and turned to face her. "I'm going to leave now."

Horror washed over her, and he rushed to add, "Not the house party. I don't think anything could incite me to leave right now."

She frowned as another thought occurred to her. "Was it that bad? The kiss?" She had to look away. "I know you've been with many women. I'm sure I could improve with practice."

She hated how her voice sounded so small and uncertain, but her suspicion that he hadn't enjoyed her kisses was beyond embarrassing.

He reached for her, grasping her upper arms and bringing her close. But it wasn't close enough for her liking.

"Your kisses..." His voice was filled with emotion. "It was unexpected. Beyond anything I've ever experienced."

She had to ask. "In a good way or a bad way?"

"In the most terrifying of ways." One corner of his mouth quirked up when he saw her confusion. "In the best of ways. Which is why I need to leave this library now while I still can."

He didn't release her right away. They stood that way for some time, staring into each other's eyes while he held onto her arms.

"Make no mistake, Iris Rowland. I want you

more than I have ever wanted anyone. But I won't take advantage of you."

She released an impatient breath, annoyed with his insistence on keeping her at a distance. He'd sent her away once before, and she hated the thought of him doing so again. She was of age to be wed. He needn't be careful with her. "If memory serves, I'm the one who led you here and asked you to kiss me."

"Yes, and I want nothing more than to bring you to my chamber and have my way with you right now. But this isn't a decision to be made lightly, in the heat of the moment. If anything more is to happen between us, I need you to be certain."

She couldn't help but take heart at his words. A very large part of her wanted to beg him to do just that, but he was right. She wasn't thinking clearly right now. But would she ever be levelheaded when it came to this man?

She followed him out from behind the bookshelf and watched him cross the room and stride to the door. The door that was still open and through which anyone could have come in while they were kissing. Or talking about making love, for that matter.

She was grateful then that at least one of them still had the presence of mind to put a halt to their very inappropriate behavior before they were caught alone together.

He turned when he reached the entrance. “I will wait for a sign from you that you wish to proceed. But be very sure about your decision, Iris. Because once I start with you, I won’t be able to stop.”

He left, and Iris realized her heart was racing. Wentworth wanted her, and for some unfathomable reason, he was acting like a gentleman. But he was still a rogue, and she knew that it would take very little to convince him that she belonged in his bed.

It wouldn’t lead to marriage of course, but she realized that she wanted him too. She didn’t think she’d change her mind, but she would take the time to consider what she needed to do next.

Lily. Her sister had married a rogue. One that had spirited her away. Iris needed to speak to her sister and get her advice.

She was heading to her sister’s room when she stopped. What if she and her husband were making love even now? Her face scrunched. She had no desire to walk in on any intimacies between Lily and Seaford.

She changed direction and made her way to her bedroom. She'd ask one of the staff to deliver a note asking Lily to come see her at her earliest convenience.

It wouldn't be soon enough.

CHAPTER 9

Wentworth waited what seemed an eternity for either Thornton or Seaford to come downstairs. He'd prefer to speak to Seaford, but if he had to, Thornton would also do.

He wanted to wait in the breakfast room but expected their wives would be with them. So he made his way to the billiard room.

It was blessedly empty. He set the table anyway in an attempt to distract himself. He didn't really need the practice, and if truth be told, the act didn't occupy his thoughts at all.

Iris had managed to embed herself under his very skin, and he was starting to suspect that he very much liked her there.

He'd just sunk the ball for what seemed like the

hundredth time when he realized he was no longer alone.

"We didn't expect to find you here so early. Did you even make it to bed last night?"

Thornton's words set his teeth on edge. Somehow he reined in the sharp retort that sprang to his lips and turned instead to put the cue stick back with the others.

When he turned, he was relieved to see that Seaford stood next to Thornton.

Seaford was examining him a little too closely, as though he could tell that Wentworth was on edge and why. "Would you like a little competition this time?"

"No. But I do need to speak to the two of you. Alone."

He moved to the door and turned the lock. When he turned back to face the pair, their expressions were carefully neutral.

Thornton spoke first. "You're bored. You needn't worry, we can make your excuses when you leave."

He clasped his hands together behind his back and braced himself for the men's reactions. "How did you know when you'd found the woman you wanted to marry?"

Seaford and Thornton exchanged glances. It was the former who asked, "Iris?"

Wentworth's calm was fast slipping away. "Yes, dammit." He jammed his hands into his coat pockets and began to pace. "I don't understand what's happening. I had a plan. Being trapped here, I was certain I'd soon come to realize I was mistaken about her. That she couldn't be nearly as interesting as I suspected. Certainly not fascinating enough to account for why my thoughts continue to circle back to our chance meeting." He stopped pacing and spun to face them. "It was a good plan."

Thornton raised a brow. "You can't get her out of your thoughts?"

Wentworth's lips twisted to the side. "No, dammit, and it's deuced inconvenient."

Seaford settled into a chair and steepled his hands at his waist. "When exactly did you meet her?"

Wentworth winced. "It was near the end of the season, during that last ball. I'd arranged to meet someone—no, not her!—in the gardens. I came across her instead."

Thornton tensed. "What happened?"

Wentworth scowled. "I didn't ravish her if that's what you're thinking. I don't need to force myself on maidens when I can have my fill of female company."

"So you what? Had a pleasant conversation with her?" Seaford's voice was surprisingly even.

"I warned her that it wasn't wise to make plans to meet someone alone in the gardens."

Thornton and Seaford looked at one another, and Wentworth all but growled. "Spare me your platitudes about my hypocrisy. I know very well the irony of what I was saying, which is why I felt it best to warn her about all the blackguards who walk among us. Men who would have no qualms taking things further than a foolish young woman searching for love would expect."

Silence descended for several seconds, and he realized he'd all but yelled that last statement. He who could find amusement in almost every situation and who never raised his voice. But just thinking about the harm that might have befallen Iris out in that garden had him wanting to tear out his hair.

It also begged a bigger question he hadn't wanted to consider: why did he care so much?

Seaford leaned forward. "I won't ask you what exactly happened out in that garden, but only because it's clear to everyone that Iris doesn't fear you. But tell me, what happened when Iris returned to the ball?"

Wentworth frowned. "This was right at the end of the season, so nothing happened."

Thornton crossed his arms over his chest and watched him in silence. It was deuced uncomfortable.

Seaford continued. "With your other paramours, why are you even here, Wentworth? I'm sure you have a mistress, and London is filled with widows right now who are trying to avoid their families."

Wentworth dropped into an armchair. "I dismissed her."

Thornton's eyes widened. "Your mistress? And what about the other women?"

He shook his head. "There haven't been any other women."

Seaford smirked. "I see the problem now. You're obsessed with thoughts of Iris."

Wentworth sprang to his feet again and began to pace. "I don't understand it. She's a mere chit of a girl. Why can't I stop thinking about her?"

Seaford's tone was serious now. "Tell me, did you keep your assignation that evening out in the gardens?"

Wentworth grimaced. “No. I sent her away.”

“Why?” Seaford prodded.

“Because I couldn’t stand it when she touched me. I allowed it at first, expecting she’d be able to erase all thoughts of Iris, but in the end I had to push her away.”

Thornton settled into the chair Wentworth had abandoned. “And after that evening?”

Wentworth faced them. “It’s a pattern that’s been repeated with every other woman. After the first few, I stopped trying.”

“But things are different with Iris,” Seaford said.

Wentworth frowned. “Yes.”

A hint of a smile touched Thornton’s lips. “She’s very beautiful.”

“And intelligent,” Seaford added.

“And witty, bewitching, damn bewildering…” Wentworth realized what he was saying. Where his thoughts were headed.

Seaford and Thornton shared another significant look. It was Seaford who spoke. “You love her.”

Wentworth shook his head. “I can’t. I’m incapable of such sentimentality.”

Thornton leaned back in the chair and grinned

at him. "You're looking at two confirmed bachelors who didn't believe in love."

Wentworth leaned back against the billiard table and frowned. "I know I'll have to marry eventually, of course. Secure the line and all that."

Seaford laughed. "That's exactly what we thought as well. But then we found ourselves bewitched by the women who are now our wives."

Wentworth folded his arms over his chest and closed his eyes as he considered their words. His thoughts had been dancing perilously close to this conclusion, but every time he considered that he might *want* to marry Iris, he pushed the idea away as quickly as it came. But the thought of another man marrying her, touching her, and bedding her…

He swore aloud.

It seemed that this Christmas he'd be giving his mother her deepest desire. News that he would soon be marrying. Because it *was* going to happen soon.

He just had to convince Iris she wouldn't be making a big mistake in accepting his suit.

CHAPTER 10

After their all-too-brief kisses in the library that morning, the world seemed bright and new. Exciting.

Iris managed to speak to her sister, and that discussion had gone better than she'd thought. She'd expected Lily to warn her to stay away from a man like Wentworth. Instead, she'd urged Iris to continue with caution—and to trust her own instincts.

Lily's husband was proof that a rake could reform his ways and become a devoted husband, but Iris didn't expect lightning to strike twice. Wentworth wasn't going to fall in love with her, let alone want to marry her.

Still, she wanted to be with him. It wouldn't

take much for her to fall in love with him, and she expected they would only have these next few days together. Despite the logical part of her mind telling her that it would be safer to guard her heart, her intuition was telling her to enjoy whatever he was willing to share with her. She could deal with a bruised heart later.

Her decision made, she wanted nothing more than to speak to him again. Like yesterday, the women and men were kept apart for much of the day. She could tell that Celia and Lily were feeling much the same way as her and wanted nothing more than to suggest they sneak into the billiard room to see what the men were up to.

It wasn't as though they didn't know how to play, after all.

Finally, it was time to dress for dinner. But today Wentworth wasn't waiting for her outside her bedchamber. Despite what he'd said in the library, she was beginning to worry about whether he'd changed his mind.

And then she saw him waiting for her at the bottom of the stairs. She didn't try to hold back her smile. The time for pretense was behind her.

Wentworth bowed over her hand and led her to the drawing room, which was already filled with guests. There was no privacy, but Iris didn't mind. Because Wentworth was being attentive. If she didn't know better, she would have thought that he was courting her.

It was impossible to miss the glances that were cast their way throughout dinner. She could all but read their thoughts as everyone tried to decipher what was happening between her and Wentworth. He was attentive but frustratingly circumspect.

Like yesterday evening, they were able to snatch a few minutes together.

"I hope it snows tomorrow," Wentworth said when they were finally alone.

Or as alone as one could be in a room filled with people.

"Are you hoping we'll be snowed in, my lord? I didn't think you such a fan of house parties."

The low timbre of his voice raced along her nerve endings when he leaned a little closer. "I am when you're in attendance."

She searched his face, telling herself that she would be a fool to search for any sign of emotional attachment from this man.

Women were gathering again by the pianoforte, and Iris's heart was beginning to race. She'd be pulled into the group soon.

She took a deep breath and pitched her voice so that it was just above a whisper. "Come to my room later."

She'd surprised him. But there was no time to hear his reply because Violet stopped in front of them.

"The two of you can chat later. Come and join us, Iris." She started to turn but spun back, as though realizing that she'd just been rude. "Of course you're also welcome to join us, my lord. We could use more men."

Iris met his gaze. "Will you be joining us?"

He winced. "My singing voice hasn't improved since the last time you asked. As for the other, nothing could keep me away."

Iris floated through the rest of the night. After carols, several guests divided into groups to play whist, while a few of the other guests took turns on the pianoforte. Iris partnered with Wentworth against Lily and Seaford for a rubber of whist. She and Wentworth won only one of the three games, but they came close on the other two.

Finally, at long last, people started bidding each other good night. Nervousness warred with excitement within her as Wentworth did the same. He didn't touch her, and nothing in his expression was untoward, but surely that in itself was a sign that he hadn't changed his mind. He was being careful so no one would suspect the fact that he'd be visiting her bedchamber tonight.

One hour later, she was beginning to worry. She'd hurried her maid along, pretending that she was tired and looking forward to turning in. Then after the young woman had left, she'd begun to pace.

Then she'd sat down to read but found she couldn't concentrate on the words.

Had Wentworth changed his mind? Or perhaps he'd been waylaid by another. What if Lily had told Seaford what might happen tonight? Her brother-in-law might have issued a warning for Wentworth to stay away.

That wouldn't do. She'd just have to go to his bedroom instead.

She was on her feet and about to open her door when she realized she didn't know where Wentworth slept. Frowning, she began to pace. Wentworth had seen her leave her bedchamber that first evening, but Violet and Clara had been with her. He might not know whose room they were leaving. Even now, he could be waiting out in the hallway for her to appear.

She rushed to her door and swung it open. She looked first one way, then the other.

Disappointment crashed through her. The hallway was empty.

And then Wentworth materialized from the shadows.

She could only smile, anticipation surging, as she waited for him to enter the room. He was silent as he turned to lock the door.

And then she was in his arms, her body pressed against the door as he ravaged her mouth in a kiss that spoke of his own impatience.

They spent several minutes that way, wrapped up in each other as they kissed their fill. She threaded her fingers through his dark hair and reveled in the feel of him pressed against her, the hard length of his arousal pressing against her belly.

Finally, he lifted his head and gazed down at her, his eyes dark with desire.

"I thought you would never open this door. I was beginning to worry this was your sister's room." He cupped her chin and traced her lower lip with a thumb. "Are you sure you wish me to stay?"

Lily had told Iris that when it was time, she would know whether she should proceed. She searched inward for a hint of doubt and could find none. Only anticipation and a sense of certainty.

She nodded. "But I'm afraid I used up my store of bravery in issuing this invitation. You need to tell me what to do."

"I'm trying to convince myself that I'm not dreaming."

He seemed so earnest, but Iris couldn't understand why. Surely there wasn't a woman alive who'd be able to resist this man.

She cupped his cheek. "I can assure you that you're not dreaming."

She wound her fingers through his hair again, enjoying the feel of the short dark strands between her fingers, and urged his head down. And then he kissed her again.

Iris was determined not to worry about the future. They would have tonight, and perhaps tomorrow night if Wentworth wasn't disappointed. When it was time to leave, they'd go their separate ways.

She would be headed to Seaford and Lily's estate, where her family was joining them for Christmas. She hoped that Wentworth would head to his own estate so he could spend Christmas with his family. But she wouldn't ask him. If he was returning to London to seek out companionship with another woman, she didn't want to know about it.

Perhaps when the season began again in a few short months, she'd be ready to move past this man. Find someone who intrigued her even a fraction as much as he did. But until that day, she was going to embrace the brief time they had together.

"Iris."

Her name was a low growl, and it sent a shiver of longing through her. She wasn't just some woman he was spending the night with. He'd been obsessed with her, curious about her, and his need was obvious in that one harshly spoken word.

She realized that she didn't know his given name.

He trailed kisses along her jaw, then settled his mouth at the side of her throat. Desire pooled low in her belly, which shocked her. She'd seen Seaford kiss Lily in a similar fashion. Had her sister also experienced this sudden onslaught of need?

"Yes, Wentworth?" She was surprised by her husky tone.

When he raised his head to stare down at her, his brows were drawn together. "That won't do."

Her thoughts were addled, and she didn't understand what she'd done wrong. "My lord?"

His frown turned into a scowl. "That's even worse. My given name is Henry."

The admission surprised her. It seemed like such an ordinary name for such an extraordinary man. "Henry." She tried it out, but now it was her turn to frown. No, that didn't suit him. "Can I call you Harry?" That seemed more casual, not quite so formal. She could imagine a Harry doing unspeakable things to her. Henry, not so much.

His smile widened into a grin. "No one has ever called me that before."

She must have overstepped. "I apologize—"

He dropped a kiss onto her mouth. "I like it. It can be your special name for me."

This was verging into dangerous territory. She couldn't have a special name for him. She was just one woman among many.

She should protest. Tell him that he didn't have to pretend with her. That she'd come to terms with the fact that they'd only be together a short time after which they'd both move on with their regular lives. Him to new adventures and other women and her to a respectable marriage to someone who would never make her feel the same way he could.

Her thoughts scrambled when he swept her into his arms and crossed the room to the bed. Instead of dropping her onto it and doing wicked things to her, he settled her onto her feet next to it.

He stared down into her eyes for several seconds before speaking. "I'm going to be careful, but you should know there will be pain."

His concern touched her. "I know what to expect, but I fear you might find me lacking."

He gripped her chin. "Never."

CHAPTER 11

She didn't believe him. Which of course made her a wise young woman. But she'd learn soon enough that he was telling her the truth.

"Am I your first?" He suspected that he knew the answer already.

She nodded. "My sister said that there are things you can do to ensure I don't fall pregnant?"

A sudden image invaded his thoughts. Iris round with their child, smiling at him. The thought should terrify him, but he was beginning to realize that Thornton and Seaford just might be correct. His feelings for Iris went far beyond desire. He wanted forever with her.

He nodded by way of answer. He wanted to tell

her that it didn't matter since he would take care of her, but he wasn't sure she'd believe him. He'd never offered false promises to a woman, but she wouldn't know that.

He would worry later how to convince her there would never be another woman for him. But first he had to go about the business of ensuring Iris became so addicted to his touch she'd never want another.

He stepped back and began to disrobe. Her eyes were wide as she watched him remove his coat and waistcoat and drop them on the floor. Then he removed his cravat and shirt, tossing both garments onto the pile. His valet would lecture him tomorrow morning about taking better care with his clothing, but right now Wentworth couldn't stop.

He enjoyed the way her eyes were glued to his chest, her mouth slightly open. It pained him to move so slowly, but he had to be sure she wanted him as much as he wanted her. That she wouldn't change her mind.

So he stood there, bare to the waist, and waited to see what she would do.

She didn't disappoint him when she settled onto the bed and leaned back on her elbows. "You may continue," she said with a wave of one hand toward his trousers.

He laughed, charmed.

He unbuttoned the fall of his trousers, his gaze fixed on her. Her breath was coming a little faster now. He wanted to tease her, but he would do that another time. He was already harder than he'd ever been in his life, and he wasn't sure how long his patience would hold.

He removed the rest of his clothing, the weight of her gaze tracing over his skin like a caress.

"I can see now what all the fuss is about."

He frowned, hating that she'd heard others gossiping about him. He wasn't surprised, not really, but the thought bothered him more than it should. Right now, here in this bedchamber, it was just the two of them. He didn't want Iris to think about anyone else.

He waited for her to look her fill. When she finally met his amused gaze, she smiled. "You can hardly blame me for being curious."

He settled onto the edge of the bed, sitting close without touching her. "Perhaps you'd do me the honor of satisfying my own curiosity."

Heat flooded her face, but her hands rose to the

ribbon that was tied at the front of her chemise, holding it in place.

He waited, but it seemed Iris might have reached the limits of her bravado. His fingers met hers, and he pulled at the ribbon, his eyes fixed on the way the fine white fabric parted, revealing her breasts.

"I'm not well endowed—"

He stopped her protest with a hungry kiss. "You're perfect, Iris."

He allowed her to take the lead, enjoying the way her gaze, then her hands wandered over his shoulders and his chest. "You're so hard."

He pushed her chemise off her shoulders and cupped her breasts. "And you, my dear, are delightfully soft."

She fell onto her back, tugging him over her, and he went willingly. His mind was filled with everything he wanted to do with this woman. But somehow he needed to slow down, or it would be over far too soon and her only memory of her first coupling would be how much it had hurt.

He shifted lower and took one breast into his mouth, delighting in her taste and in the way she gasped and threaded her fingers through his hair. He spent some time there, going from one breast to the other, feeling the racing of her heart under his mouth and hands. But he wasn't a patient man, and his body was already threatening to spill. He'd already waited forever for Iris.

He trailed lower, kissing her belly as he tugged the chemise down below her hips. Somehow he kept from tearing the fabric as he shifted to the side and dragged it down her legs.

He rose up onto his arms then, looking down the length of her body. Iris bit her lower lip as she waited for him.

He hadn't thought it possible for a woman to take his breath away, but Iris did just that. And it wasn't because she was laid out in wanton abandon. No, he'd had his fill of women who were comfortable with their sexuality. But Iris's trust humbled him. He was her first, and God willing, he was going to be her last. The only man to see her this way.

"Do you trust me?" Her actions said that she did, but he needed to hear the words.

"Yes."

"Good girl. Now open your legs for me."

It took her a few seconds, but with a nod and a tremulous smile, she did just that.

And then he showed her just how he could

pleasure her without any pain. First with his fingers, and then with his mouth. He didn't think he'd ever be able to get enough of this woman. The way she gasped in shock, then moaned in pleasure.

And her whispered "Harry" when he covered her mound with his mouth had him almost spilling against the sheets.

It didn't take him long to bring her to her first release that way, and then he moved into place over her. She kissed him with abandon, not caring that he tasted of her.

He pushed into her, spearing into her with one quick thrust, and then stilled once her body gripped him.

He'd heard her gasp of pain, but they'd needed to move past that part quickly. He'd never taken a woman's maidenhead, and he was probably bungling the entire affair, but somehow he found the strength to hold still.

Her teeth had clamped down on the skin of his shoulder, and he wondered for a moment if she'd drawn blood. Given that he'd breached her like an inexperienced youth, he wasn't about to complain if she had.

Because the slight sting of her bite was nothing

compared to the bliss of being inside her. Mingled with the torture of not moving.

He kissed her, hoping to bring her back to pleasure. She tore her mouth from his after a few seconds and stared at him.

"You're so big."

He groaned and closed his eyes. This woman was trying to kill him.

"Does it still hurt?"

A small vee formed between her brows. "I don't think so."

He took a deep breath and summoned the willpower to draw out of her body slowly before easing back into her.

Her eyes closed, and her mouth dropped open.

He watched her carefully. "How about now?"

"Do that again."

He let out a relieved breath. "With pleasure, my lady."

And he made love to her then, moving in and out of her with care. Never before had he taken equal pleasure in watching the joy he wrung from his bed partner. Oh, he made sure they experienced pleasure—he wasn't that selfish—but their satisfaction had never served to intensify his own.

But with Iris… Each time she moaned and

clutched at him, the way her legs came up to embrace him… He felt as though his heart was going to explode.

Finally she came, and somehow he had the presence of mind to swallow her cries of pleasure with his kiss. When he pulled out of her to finish, he vowed that one day, soon, he wouldn't need to take such precautions. Because Iris was his.

He shifted onto his side, enjoying the way she came with him and settled into his embrace.

Her fingers traced over his back, his hip, and then she dropped a kiss onto his chest and looked up at him.

"Thank you, Harry. I hope…" She looked away, and he waited. Finally, after taking a deep breath, she met his gaze again. "When we leave here, I hope you think of me fondly from time to time."

He rolled over her again, caging her body under his as he stared into her eyes.

"I'm not even close to being done with you."

CHAPTER 12

Iris woke with a smile on her face. Last night had been glorious. Despite the fact they'd only made love once—she'd told him she was too sore to do so again—he'd spent most of the night with her.

He'd slipped out just before dawn, dropping a kiss onto her forehead before leaving.

She rolled over and buried her face in the pillow that still smelled like him. She couldn't name the scent, but it was now her favorite.

She'd been dreaming of him before she woke, and she closed her eyes, trying to recapture the final images. They were back in that garden where they'd met, and he was saying something to her…

Her eyes sprang open. He'd told her that he loved her in the dream. Even worse, she'd vowed that she would never love another man.

She sprang from the bed and stared down at the mussed sheets in horror.

She was in love with Wentworth.

She began to pace. This was terrible. They would only have one more night together, and then they'd both be leaving. Her to join her family in celebrating Christmas with Lily at Seaford's estate and him to London.

And other women.

No, this wouldn't do. She couldn't be in love with the man. She was behaving like any other sentimental young fool. Her emotions were all tangled up because Wentworth had been kind to her, passionate, and generous.

And no man would ever be able to compete.

She'd made a terrible mistake.

She sank down onto the bed again and reached for his pillow, hugging it to her chest. No, it hadn't been a mistake. Unwise, perhaps, but she didn't regret being with him.

But one thing was painfully clear—she couldn't spend another night with him. Her heart already ached with the knowledge she couldn't have him. If she allowed herself to spend another night with him, her heart would never recover.

CHAPTER 13

Iris was avoiding him, and he didn't know why.

After spending most of the day apart, she'd been distant with him over dinner. Cordial. Polite.

He hated it.

When the meal was over, he watched her leave the dining room with the other women. Then he rose and rounded the table. He approached Thornton, then Seaford, and inclined his head to one side of the room.

They weren't alone, but he no longer cared about discretion. If the others wanted to listen in on their conversation, they were welcome. "Iris is ignoring me," he said.

Thornton frowned. "What did you do?"

"Nothing!" He winced. He lowered his voice so it was barely above a whisper before adding, "We were together last night, but I swear upon my honor that it was consensual. *She* invited *me* to her bedchamber."

Seaford raised one brow. "And?"

"It was glorious. Incredible. The best night of my life. But now she's barely speaking to me, and I don't understand why."

Both men folded their arms across their chests as though they'd coordinated the movement. It was Seaford who spoke. "What are your intentions? Are you disappointed because you were hoping to spend another night with her before going on your merry way?"

Wentworth scowled. "No." He realized he'd spoken far too loudly when several heads turned in his direction. "Iris is mine. I want to marry her."

Thornton's eyes widened in surprise. Seaford, however, clapped him on the back. He didn't appear to be surprised by the outburst. "You left her satisfied?"

"Of course. I need to speak to her."

Thornton let out a resigned breath. "We can hardly allow you to spirit her away. But perhaps our wives can lure her away from the ballroom so you can speak to her."

Relief flooded through him. "Thank you. I am forever in your debt."

"Don't thank us yet," Seaford said. "The Rowland women can be quite stubborn."

They made him wait an interminable quarter of an hour before announcing it was time to join the women for the evening.

After entering the ballroom, Wentworth scanned the clusters of women. He found Iris sitting between two older women. She would have heard the men enter the room—several were arguing about whether they would wake up to snow tomorrow—but she didn't glance their way.

Iris was definitely pulling away from him, and he needed to find out why so he could fix the situation. If she were any other woman, he would have celebrated the fact that there would be no awkward displays, simply a mutual parting of the ways after an enjoyable night together. But Iris's distance left him feeling as though he were missing a part of himself.

He moved to one side of the room, careful to keep her within his sight lest she change her mind and give him a sign that she wanted him to approach her. But she concentrated on the two women sitting next to her to the exclusion of all else.

True to their word, Thornton and Seaford approached their wives. After a short conversation, during which both women glanced his way, Viscountess Thornton and the Countess of Seaford approached Iris and said something to her. Probably asked her to go with them since Iris rose and followed the women from the room.

She didn't look at him, but it was clear she knew exactly where he was standing. It was the one part of the room she avoided looking at.

Seaford approached. "They're taking her just down the hall. We'll stand by the door to delay anyone from leaving the room, but we won't be able to bar the exit for long."

The constriction around his heart was beginning to ease. "Thank you."

He slipped from the room and spotted the trio of women clustered down the hall a fair distance away. Iris was clutching her sister's hand and whispering something to her.

He started toward the group, his steps faltering when Iris turned to look at him. The pain on her face tore at him.

He inclined his head to the two women. “Thank you for understanding and agreeing to give us a moment to speak.”

Seaford’s wife frowned. “Have a care with my sister’s heart.”

He nodded.

Iris watched them go, the expression on her face forlorn.

Somehow he kept from reaching for her. “Are you angry with me? Did I fumble last night horribly?”

She met his gaze then. “No, Harry. You were wonderful.”

He took heart from the fact that she wasn’t insisting on formality between them. “So why are you ignoring me now?”

She folded her arms around her waist as though he was hurting her. “I’m falling in love with you.”

Her admission left him stunned. He’d hoped for as much, but given the distance she was trying to erect between them, he feared he’d done something to make her hate him.

“Just so,” she said, her voice shaky. As though she were trying to hold back tears. “It’s a disaster. It seems that I am unable to conduct a short affair with you. I only ask that you respect my wishes and not press me further on this."

She wasn't making any sense. "Because you love me."

"Yes. And you don't engage in love affairs. Just physical ones."

One corner of his mouth lifted. "What if I decided that I could?"

She searched his eyes, looking for something. Whatever it was, she didn't find it, because she shook her head. "My heart would never survive. We can't continue on this path. If I'm to get past the inconvenient feelings I've developed for you, we need to end things now."

She brushed past him, and he watched her hurry down the hall. When she reached the entrance, she stopped and took a deep breath. Then, shoulders back and head held high, she entered the ballroom.

Iris loved him. But she was leaving because she needed to guard her heart.

He couldn't have that, so of course he followed. When he entered the room, she was standing with her cousin and sister again.

"Iris Rowland."

His voice rang out throughout the room, and

every eye turned to him. Everyone except Iris. She stiffened, but she didn't turn to look at him.

It seemed he was going to need to make a spectacle of himself. It was a good thing he didn't really care what everyone was thinking. He only cared about the woman he loved.

"Please look at me, Iris."

Some were starting to whisper, but they were quickly shushed. No one wanted to miss what was happening.

Iris turned, and he crossed the room to stand before her.

"I can't honor your request because, you see, I love you. And I want only you."

Iris's eyes widened in shock. Then she shook her head.

Determination coursed through him, and he dropped onto one knee. When he reached for her hand, she didn't resist.

"Iris Rowland, would you do me the honor of becoming my wife?"

She stared at him. "But…" She swallowed. "Are you certain?"

He scanned the other guests who'd now all moved closer to surround them in a tight circle.

When he met her gaze again, a look of wonder was starting to form on her face.

"It seems you bewitched me that night we met. Please put me out of my misery and say you'll marry me."

She was nodding now. "Yes, I will. Of course I will."

He rose to his feet and pulled her into his arms.

"I can't believe you made a public declaration," she murmured against his jaw before placing a soft kiss there. "You won't be able to take it back now."

He stared down at her, a feeling like nothing he'd ever experienced settling over him. Joy. Certainty.

Happiness.

"I guess that means you're stuck with me now." And then he kissed her because there was nothing like a public scandal to bind a woman to your side. Just in case she was beginning to have any second thoughts.

EPILOGUE

Christmas Eve

Wentworth had managed to convince Seaford to invite him to his estate to celebrate Christmas with his family and the Rowlands. It was actually a practical suggestion since Wentworth still had to ask Iris's father for permission to marry his daughter. Technically, he should have done that before proclaiming his love to a full room, but he'd been a little desperate.

He wasn't surprised that he and Iris weren't allowed to share his carriage. Still, he couldn't help his sullen mood when Seaford joined him, telling him that the women would enjoy chatting together in the other carriage.

But he'd had his revenge when the first flakes of snow started to fall when they reached the estate. He suspected Seaford had planned to ask him to leave after Christmas Day, but it seemed nature was on Wentworth's side.

Mr. Rowland's surprise that there would be another guest for Christmas had passed quickly. With a wry comment about how his daughters seemed to be making a habit of bringing gentlemen home for Christmas, he led Wentworth to the library. Rowland wasn't nearly as thorough in questioning him about his intentions as he should have been, but he did grant his permission for them to wed.

Everything seemed to be going his way. Except, as had been his lot in life since he first stumbled upon Iris out in that garden, it seemed he would have to wait even longer to claim her fully. Three weeks for the banns to be read in the parish church. Fortunately, his mother had written back to assure him that she would see to it that they were also read at the parish on his country seat.

All too soon, Iris would be returning home with her father and sister, and then Wentworth would have to wait those three weeks here at Seaford's estate. Because while Rowland might be pleased about his daughter's upcoming marriage, he clearly wasn't foolish enough to allow them to remain under the same roof for weeks on end.

Which meant they'd have to make the most of the little time they had together until they were separated.

Grateful for the note Iris had slipped into his hands with directions, he was able to steal into her room again that night. Everyone knew what was happening, but that didn't mean they shouldn't be discreet.

After making love, they lay together. Iris's head rested on his chest, and he ran a hand along her spine. A bone-deep contentment settled through him. After they married, he would have to ensure she slept in his bed every night.

Iris lifted her head then, a small frown on her face.

"What's the matter, love? Surely you're not already tired of our lovemaking."

Iris sighed. "I'm worried about Papa."

His hand stilled on her back. "Your father seems well. Happy, even."

"Yes, and that is most unusual. He doesn't come to Viscount Thornton's house party because he finds it draining to be with so many people over several days."

He could understand that. Some people didn't like to socialize. "So why are you worried?"

"Because he was here when we arrived. The dowager countess invited him to spend time here while we were away… and he accepted! Last year he refused the invitation to spend Christmas Day here, but now here we all are. I think he might be lonely. Which makes me feel horrible for abandoning him."

He could imagine what had enticed Rowland to visit Seaford's mother while she was home alone. They were being circumspect, but he caught the way they seemed to light up when in each other's presence. And there had been a few significant glances when the older couple thought no one was looking. If the pair weren't yet lovers, they were well on their way.

If Wentworth wasn't mistaken, Seaford also knew what his mother was up to. But how much would Iris want to know? He had no proof, just supposition, and this wasn't his secret to tell. It was no one's business if the older couple wanted to spend time together. And he had no way of knowing just how far they'd gone when it came to comforting one another.

"You shouldn't feel guilty. Lily is already married, and soon you will be as well. Violet might find someone during this next season. It makes sense that he wants to spend time with a family who is near."

Iris's frown deepened. "If he becomes lonely, can we invite him to live with us?"

He started stroking his hand along her spine again, enjoying the way she leaned into his touch unselfconsciously. "Of course. But I think that your father likes it here."

Iris examined him, and he realized that he was on the verge of giving away Rowland's secret love affair. It was time to change the subject. "You need to speak to your cousin about next year's Christmas party. It is ridiculous how her mother-in-law insists on keeping the men and women separated all day."

Iris's brow smoothed. "I thought the men preferred that."

He rolled her onto her back and hovered over her. "This man certainly didn't. And I can guarantee that Thornton and Seaford didn't either."

Iris giggled. He loved hearing her laugh. "I take

it that means we'll be coming down next year for the Christmas house party?"

The things he did for love. But gazing down at the woman who would soon be his wife, he knew that he would spend a lifetime trying to make her happy.

❄

THANK YOU FOR READING *A ROGUE FOR CHRISTMAS*. I hope you enjoyed Iris and Wentworth's story. Book 4 in the Christmas Scandals series will be available next year and will tell Violet Rowland's story. (Hint: We'll learn who Violet is writing all those letters to!) Sign up for my newsletter (suzannamedeiros.com/newsletter) if you want to stay up to date on what I'm doing.

❄

TURN THE PAGE TO READ AN EXCERPT FROM THE latest release in my Landing a Lord series—*Courting the Earl*. You won't want to miss it if you like books with the following tropes: forbidden love, friends to lovers, a spinster heroine and a reluctant hero!

EXCERPT - COURTING THE EARL

Eleanor Pearson is distressed by the forbidden attraction she feels for her cousin's betrothed. But she vows to ignore her fascination with the attractive earl and do whatever she can to ensure her cousin's marriage takes place.

The Earl of Hargrove has no intention of marrying anytime soon. He sets out on a mission of his own to end the surprise arrangement his father revealed to him only on his deathbed.

It doesn't take him long to realize that Eleanor could be the key to convincing the younger woman to end the betrothal. But his attraction to her threatens his determination to remain a bachelor.

Unlike the growing crowds of people filling the large ballroom, Geoffrey wasn't thrilled to be attending the Clarington ball. But since this was the battlefield upon which his current war would be waged, here he was. Along with what seemed to be every other member of society minus his sister and brother-in-law. Abigail was quite far into her pregnancy and went to bed early most evenings, so he'd have to face tonight on his own.

He'd considered making himself odious to Miss Lydia Pearson so the young woman would beg her father to end the betrothal but had quickly discarded that plan. If he were the only one affected by his actions, he would have no issue acting the cad to drive her away. But he needed to consider his sister. Causing a scandal would hurt her far more than it would him.

Viscount Holbrook sidled up next to him and clapped him on the shoulder. "Try not to look as though you're being led to your death."

Geoffrey scowled at him, which caused Holbrook to chuckle. He wouldn't admit as much, but he was glad he wasn't entirely alone.

By unspoken agreement, they moved off to the edge of the room. Most people were congregating closer to the entrance so they could scrutinize each new guest as they were announced.

Holbrook was busy examining the guests who were already present. "Tell me about this young woman you'll be marrying."

Geoffrey clasped his hands behind his back. Of course Holbrook knew about that. The man seemed to know everything. Since an announcement wouldn't be made until the end of the season, he must have heard about the betrothal from Abigail.

He scanned the ballroom again. He hadn't heard Appleby's family being announced, but then he hadn't really been paying attention as the butler droned on with the seemingly unending list of guests. He hadn't been there long, and he was already tempted to escape to the card room.

"Did my sister send you here to keep an eye on me?"

Holbrook chuckled. "Believe it or not, it was her husband."

Geoffrey had a hard time imagining that conversation. Holbrook seemed to go out of his way to annoy Geoffrey's brother-in-law, flirting with Abigail outrageously whenever Cranston was present.

"I'm amazed he even speaks to you."

Holbrook shrugged. "We've come to an understanding. And most importantly, he loves and trusts his wife. Even if I wanted to try my hand at tempting her away…"

Geoffrey scowled at the man.

One corner of Holbrook's mouth quirked up. "I consider your sister a friend, nothing more. I had a duty to look out for her when my bastard of a great-uncle died and left his widow with very little to provide for herself and her daughter."

"That's not how Cranston tells the story of your *friendship*."

Holbrook chuckled. "Cranston was being willfully stubborn about his wife. Everyone but her could see he was obsessed with her. I did what I could to make him realize that he had to stop pushing her away."

Geoffrey could just imagine how that went. "I'm surprised the man didn't call you out."

Holbrook winced. "Would you believe that I sought him out and threatened to call him out if he hurt your sister? This was before they were married of course."

Geoffrey couldn't hold back a bark of laughter. How had he never heard this story? "My brother-in-law is a crack shot. He would have killed you."

Holbrook rubbed a hand over his jaw. "I realize now that I came perilously close to meeting my death after issuing that threat. But that's all in the past. We've reached a truce. He loves your sister, and he realizes now that my interest in her was never romantic. Which is why he told me about your situation."

Geoffrey's jaw clenched, and his eyes darted to one of the exits he'd made a point of noting after arriving. He could still slip out to the card room.

Holbrook moved in front of him. "Tell me you're not planning to cause a scene. There's already enough talk swirling around about your sister. Any scandal you cause to escape this betrothal will impact her."

Geoffrey blew out a harsh breath. Was this why Cranston had asked Holbrook to approach him this evening? Yes, rumors were swirling about Abigail and her daughter, Gemma. His niece had Cranston's eyes. Anyone who met the girl knew immediately that her current husband was her biological father.

There had been much speculation about whether she'd knowingly tried to pass another man's child off as belonging to her deceased husband, the former Viscount Holbrook. Of course, many knew that Baron Cranston had been serving in the army for years and had only recently given up his commission.

Gossip seemed to be split evenly. Men tended to believe Abigail had been willfully dishonest in the whole matter and had deceived her first husband. Women, on the other hand, believed she'd had no choice but to marry someone else when she'd found herself with child after the father had gone off to join the army.

The worst of the speculation was quashed when Cranston's friends had given their unconditional support to the couple after they married. While Cranston might have been away from England for nearly a decade, he'd somehow acquired quite a few friends in high places. Men most of society didn't want to offend.

So while the rumors had all but abated, that wouldn't remain the case if Geoffrey caused another scandal while attempting to get out of this infernal betrothal.

"Society has never been fair to women. My sister has suffered enough, and I won't do anything to endanger the peace she's found."

He became aware of a hush that had fallen over the ballroom and turned to look at the entrance. He shouldn't have been surprised to find none other than Lydia Pearson standing there, surrounded by her family. Her parents were grinning, basking in the way everyone seemed to be taken with their daughter. Lydia's introduction to society was going just as they'd expected.

He inclined his head toward the entrance. "They're here now."

Holbrook turned to take in the spectacle. Mercifully, he kept his voice low when he spoke. "Your future wife is definitely beautiful. Everyone is staring at her as though no one else exists."

Geoffrey's eyes moved over the crowd, and he realized the man wasn't exaggerating. Conversation had started again, but gazes were following the family.

He watched as Lord Appleby whispered in his wife's ear before breaking away to join another group of men. When they turned to one of the exits as a group, Geoffrey wanted to groan. So much for escaping to the card room at some point. The last thing he wanted was another lecture from Appleby about how he should be following the man's daughter around like a stray looking for a new owner.

Lady Appleby led her two charges toward a group of women. When he glanced at Holbrook again, he was still watching the women with interest.

"Did Cranston tell you that the betrothal can be broken if both parties are in agreement?"

Holbrook nodded. "He mentioned something to that effect. That's why he's worried you'll try to cause a scandal and force their hand."

Geoffrey frowned. "It's comforting that my brother-in-law considers me such a reprobate and believes I'll act without any consideration about how it will impact my sister."

Holbrook clapped him on the shoulder. "Cranston is being overprotective. Plus he doesn't really know you."

Geoffrey lifted one brow. "And you do?"

Holbrook grinned. "Not yet, no. But we can remedy that. Become allies."

He examined the viscount. He imagined that as

a great nephew to the previous viscount, Holbrook hadn't expected to inherit the title. Still, the man was an easygoing fellow and people seemed to like him. He couldn't imagine he was in desperate need of allies or friends.

Unless… "You have my permission to try to lure Miss Pearson away. She's a beautiful young woman, and I understand your interest."

Holbrook barked out a surprised laugh. "I'm in no hurry to wed, but that was a good attempt on your part. Still, I could be tempted to get to know the older Miss Pearson better."

Geoffrey turned to examine the woman in question. Eleanor Pearson. He'd scarce noticed her during that first meeting when all he'd wanted was to escape that drawing room and all the women's expectant stares. But he was definitely noticing her now, and he realized Holbrook was correct.

It was impossible to miss how much her appearance had improved, and he couldn't help but wonder if she'd purposely dressed in an unflattering manner that morning. She'd been stiff, wearing an awful gown that had made her skin appear sallow. He'd actually thought she was much older than her cousin. Watching her now as she laughed at something Lydia said, he realized she was much closer to his own age.

She was actually very attractive. She didn't possess the delicate beauty of her cousin. No, Eleanor Pearson's beauty was very different but nonetheless undeniable. There was something earthy about her with her dark hair and dark eyes. She was tall, towering over her petite cousin. And her age might allow her a measure of freedom that her younger cousin wouldn't have.

Eleanor Pearson might very well be a woman worth getting to know better. But her intimate acquaintance with his *betrothed*—how he hated that word—meant that Geoffrey would never be able to get to know her intimately. Still, she might become something of an ally. Maybe he could elicit her assistance in convincing Lydia to consider ending the betrothal and marrying someone else.

He circled the room for the next hour, unwilling to fall into the role assigned to him by his father and Appleby. And he certainly wasn't going to be one of the crowd of men, both young and old, who were clamoring for a space on Lydia Pearson's dance card. If she wanted to dance with him, she would save a dance. If not, he wouldn't mourn the loss of the opportunity.

He could feel Lady Appleby's eyes on him as he greeted his brother-in-law's close friends, the Marquess of Lowenbrock and Viscount Ashford. Both men hadn't abandoned their wives as Lord Appleby had done, and it seemed that they, too, were happily married.

That fact had surprised him when Cranston assured him it was possible to marry for love. Geoffrey knew that most marriages made among the ton followed the pattern his father had set for both his betrothal and his sister's first marriage.

He spent some time speaking to several of the acquaintances he'd made during his weeks in London. Some he knew from his time in school, and some he'd met at White's. He avoided the men his father had considered friends, however. He had no desire to be reminded of the man.

During that hour, he watched what was happening with Lydia and Eleanor. Lady Appleby had abandoned the pair soon after their arrival and had spent the time glaring at him and gossiping with a group of older women.

Apparently it was Eleanor's role to act as Lydia's chaperone so the girl's parents could enjoy the evening with others. He filed away that information in case it should prove useful.

Finally, after an hour had passed, he approached the two Miss Pearsons between sets.

Lydia had just joined her cousin after her last partner had left her side with what appeared to be great reluctance. It bothered him that no one had asked Eleanor to partner with them. He'd caught the wistful look in her eyes as she'd watched her young cousin dance. He couldn't say why, but he felt compelled to make up for their oversight.

Eleanor saw him approach and leaned down to whisper in her cousin's ear. Lydia turned to him with a smile and dipped into a curtsy when he reached them.

"It is good to see you, my lord. I was just telling my cousin that I didn't think you were here tonight."

Of course she didn't. She probably imagined he would elbow all other would-be suitors out of the way just to reach her side as soon as she'd been announced.

"Well, here I am."

His smile was aimed at both women. Lydia giggled, but a quick glance at Eleanor told him she wasn't amused. A slight frown had formed between her brows.

"I was speaking with friends, and when I realized you were here, you were caught up with others. I don't suppose you saved a dance for me?"

"Of course. Mama told me to save the supper dance for you."

She offered him her card, and he scribbled his name on the indicated line. He hoped his smile didn't appear false as he murmured something about looking forward to it. Then he turned to Eleanor Pearson.

"And you, Miss Pearson? I hope you have room on your dance card."

Color rose on the woman's cheeks. "I hadn't planned to dance—"

Lydia cut her off. "Oh, you must, Ellie. I hate the idea of your standing here watching me have all the fun. Acting as my chaperone doesn't mean you can't also enjoy yourself tonight."

"Well, perhaps just one dance."

"Excellent," he said before she could change her mind. "I will come collect you when it is time."

He gave them both a polite bow and then turned to leave, pretending to forget that he hadn't signed the woman's card. He was sure there would be a waltz at some point, and he'd return to collect her then. Better to ambush her than to risk Miss

Eleanor Pearson finding a way to avoid waltzing with him.

He smiled as he realized he was looking forward to that dance very much.

BOOKS BY SUZANNA MEDEIROS

Dear Stranger

Forbidden in February

(A Year Without a Duke multi-author series)

Anthologies:

The Novellas: A Collection

Hathaway Heirs: Books 1-4

Landing a Lord: Books 1-3

Landing a Lord series:

Dancing with the Duke

Loving the Marquess

Beguiling the Earl

The Unaffected Earl

The Unsuitable Duke

The Unexpected Marquess

The Unwilling Viscount

The Baron's Return

Courting the Earl

Tempting the Viscount (Coming next!)

Christmas Scandals series:

A Viscount for Christmas

A Highwayman for Christmas

A Rogue for Christmas

Hathaway Heirs series:

Lady Hathaway's Proposal

Lord Hathaway's Bride

Captain Hathaway's Dilemma

Miss Hathaway's Wish

❄

For more information please visit the author's website:

suzannamedeiros.com/books

ABOUT SUZANNA

USA Today bestselling author Suzanna Medeiros was born and raised in Toronto, Canada. Her love for the written word led her to pursue a degree in English Literature from the University of Toronto. She went on to earn a Bachelor of Education degree but graduated at a time when no teaching jobs were available. After working at a number of interesting places, including a federal inquiry, a youth probation office, and the Office of the Fire Marshal of Ontario, she decided to pursue her first love—writing.

Suzanna is married to her own hero and is the proud mother of twin daughters. She is an avowed romantic who enjoys spending her days writing love stories.

She would like to thank her parents for showing her that love at first sight and happily ever after really do exist.

To learn about Suzanna Medeiros's future books (and to receive a bonus short story!) sign up for her newsletter:
suzannamedeiros.com/newsletter

Visit her website:
suzannamedeiros.com

Or visit her on Facebook:
facebook.com/AuthorSuzannaMedeiros

Printed in Great Britain
by Amazon

33598565R00083